Half a Life

HALF A LIFE
AND OTHER STORIES

by Kirill Bulychev

TRANSLATED FROM THE RUSSIAN BY
Helen Saltz Jacobson

MACMILLAN PUBLISHING CO., INC.
NEW YORK
COLLIER MACMILLAN PUBLISHERS
LONDON

Macmillan Publishing Co., Inc.
866 Third Avenue, New York, N.Y. 10022
Collier Macmillan Canada, Ltd.

Library of Congress Cataloging in Publication Data

Bulychev, Kirill Vsevolodovich.
    Half a life, and other stories.

    Translation of selections from Lîûdi kak lîûdi and Chudesa v Guslîàre.
    CONTENTS: Half a life.—I was the first to find you.—Protest.—May I please speak to Nina? [etc.]
    1. Science fiction, Russian. I. Title.
PZ4.B93654Hal [PG3479.4.U56] 891.7'3'42 77-8403
ISBN 0-02-518030-4

FIRST PRINTING 1977

Printed in the United States of America

Contents

Introduction

THERE is a rule—admittedly flexible, and by and large unwritten—that in fiction "you must" have an angle-character, a single subjective point of view. The purpose of this is to make it possible for the reader to identify with one of the characters and (depending on the skill of the narrator) to leave the story with the feeling that the events really happened to him, rather than that the story is merely something read or observed. Most Western short fiction follows this convention: one character in a story *feels* frightened or angry or passionate, and has thoughts and memories which we share. All others *do* and *say* frightened or angry or passionate things and speak their thoughts to the reader or to each other in the reader's presence; the reader is not permitted inside anyone's head but the protagonist's. In longer fiction the point of view may shift from one character to another, but usually only within the confines of a chapter or section. Within each of these, the convention is consistently maintained.

In much modern European fiction, and noticeably in East European fiction, there is a departure from this particular "you must." The writer's approach is often reportorial, even cinematic, and the eyes through which the action is seen can be anyone's, even for a line or two. It is an interesting development, and to anyone conditioned to Russian literature through Dostoevsky and Gogol and expecting heavily convoluted, highly subjective narration, it is most engaging. It makes for a swift-moving, lean style and commands that elusive quality called "audience participation" without demanding it. Have you ever been annoyed by background music in the cinema—the mechanical assumption that the sudden appearance of a glittering knife demands a sting from the violin section, with addenda of oboe and French horn? I do not wish to be told how I must feel about a scene. Give me a dark misty street, a girl walking alone, and put on the sound track only her footsteps and those of someone unseen. Send the orchestra home. I will know how I feel, what I feel, about the situation without the assistance of Orpheus.

This, then, is the special texture of Kirill Bulychev's work, as exemplified by the stories you are about to enjoy. He will tell you what is happening, and to whom. He will not go into great detail about personalities; it will be quite clear what sort of people they are by the way they do the things they do, say the things they say. He will give you a glimpse into this mind and into that one, to suit his own convenience and sense of efficiency; and how you feel about it is absolutely up to you.

His approach to the science-fictional aspects of his stories reveals the same economy. If you need the technological data about his space ship drives, about orbits and trajectories, about intergalactic communications devices and artificial gravities, then write your own manuals. Bulychev will give you a single assumption: that there is an expedition to alien planets. Or that there is an hypnotic technique capable of penetrating amnesia induced by profound shock. Or that your own telephone might, by inexplicable accident, cross the barrier of time. He is not concerned with ways and means, nuts and bolts. He is concerned, and profoundly so, with people. This is to be applauded. There is certainly nothing wrong with handbooks and data readouts, except when they masquerade as fiction—a lesson which many of Bulychev's colleagues on both sides of all oceans seem not to have learned. There would seem to be a confusion in their minds between science and technology. Science fiction is without doubt the mythology of our era. The only enduring myths of the past are those which deal (actually or by analogy) with human actions and aspirations—that is to say, with human self-knowledge. I know of no lasting legend which deals with the exact voltage of Jove's thunderbolts, or whether or not Bifrost was a suspension bridge. The word "science" derives from a Latin term which means "knowledge." If the best and most enduring fiction is that which deals with people (and it is), then the best and most enduring science fiction is that which deals with the knowledge and self-knowledge of people. Technology is the environment of our era, and to the degree that its impact adds to our knowledge and self-knowledge, it is legitimately a part of our myth. It is not, however, the whole myth, and Bulychev knows this well.

There is one other aspect of Kirill Bulychev's technique that is worth noting. There is an artist whom you might encounter at a carnival who, with a sheet of black paper and a pair of sharp scissors, can make a silhouette portrait in just a few minutes. After it is mounted on a card and you walk away pleased, it is easy to forget that in the artist's wastebasket there now exists an equally accurate portrait, delineated not where your face is, but by where it is not. Bulychev is well aware of this technique and uses it adroitly, making his point not by what he says and shows, but by what he does not say and does not show. I venture to say that what will stay most with you once you have experienced the extraordinary title story of this collection is not the towering courage, compassion, and resourcefulness of the woman Natasha, nor the uniqueness of her terrifying adventure, but the even more terrifying, regrettably

ix

commonplace statement of human values, embodied in the last few paragraphs. Here is the rounding, the completion of Natasha's epic, the place where its trajectory returns it to the planet and people from which it began. Yet nobody cares, not really —except an aging schoolteacher, Natasha's granddaughter, yet even for her, Natasha is a remote figure, hardly a real person at all. Everyone else has other concerns. That this should be so is frightening to contemplate—and it is so.

Much the same thing applies to "I Was the First to Find You" when the exultant voice over the radio bypasses loss and grief and pain and hardship to imply its own petty and greedy set of values. Bulychev does not preach about this; he simply lays it down and lets you look at it, as he does in "Red Deer, White Deer"—a picture which has no caption because it needs none.

Then there's "First Layer of Memory," an intriguing, and most suspenseful, story about transferring personalities. "May I Please Speak to Nina?" and "Snowmaiden" are two moving love stories with the most interesting common denominator, though they are very different in all other aspects: the lovers may not touch one another. In one case it is impossible, in the other, dangerous and painful. One is tempted, perhaps inexcusably, to pry into this coincidence. Is it a product of contemporary Russian mores? Is it the reflection of something of the author's, something, perhaps, that he decries and would change? Or is there no common denominator at all beyond the accidental similarity of two excellent story ideas?

Anyway, meet some modern Soviet science fiction. Meet Kirill Bulychev. I have a feeling you'll like one another.

Theodore Sturgeon
Los Angeles, 1977

Half a Life

Half a Life

A S H O R T distance above Kalyazin, where the Volga, contained by a high left bank, flows around a wide, sharp bend, lies a large pine-covered island.

On three sides it is washed by the Volga; on the fourth it is open to a straight channel formed when the dam was built in Uglich and the water level rose. Beyond the island and the channel, there is another pine forest. From the water it appears dark, dense, and endless. Actually, it isn't that large or that dense. Since the roads and paths crossing it have a sand foundation, they are always dry, even after a rain.

One such road skirts the edge of the forest along a rye field and reaches to the water's edge opposite the island. On Sundays in the summertime, when the weather was pleasant, busloads of vacationers would drive along it to the channel, where they would fish and sunbathe. Frequently motorboats and

1

yachts would anchor by the shore near the road; silver and orange tents could be seen from the water. But the island attracted many more tourists than the mainland. Under the illusion that the island would give them solitude, they would search painstakingly for a bit of earth between their tents. Immediately after disembarking, they would clear cans and other litter from the campsite and, convinced that such a careless attitude toward nature was nothing short of barbaric, would curse the previous occupants for the mess left behind. This did not deter them from themselves leaving empty cans, bottles, and paper litter on the shore when they broke camp. In the evening the tourists would light campfires and drink tea, but unlike hikers who limited their gear to the capacity of their backpacks, they neither sang nor caroused. They usually camped in family groups, with children, dogs, an enormous quantity of food, and primus stoves for cooking.

The morose, one-armed forest ranger, who often swam in the river at the end of the road, had learned to accept the tourists. He knew that his tourists were responsible people; they always doused their fires with water or stamped them out. The one-armed ranger would shed his jacket with its oak-leaf insignia, slip off his shoes and trousers, and enter the water cautiously, probing the bottom with his foot for broken bottles or sharp stones. Waist deep, he would stop, take a deep breath, and plunge in. He used a sidestroke, propelling himself with his lone arm. Usually Natasha and Olenka remained on shore. Natasha would wash dishes in the river because the forester's house, on that end of the road, did not have a well. If she finished rinsing them before the forester emerged from the water, she would sit on a rock and wait for him, gazing at the chain of islands on the other side of the channel. For some reason it reminded her of a city street at night and evoked in her a strong desire to run off to Leningrad or Moscow. When Natasha saw that the ranger had finished, she would wade in the river up to her knees and hand him the empty buckets, which he would fill where the water was deeper and cleaner.

If tourists appeared nearby, the ranger would clutch his

jacket to his chest and stroll over to their campfire. He tried not to frighten people, spoke gently and politely to them, and always presented his left profile so the scar on his cheek would not be seen.

On the way back, he would stop to pick up litter and all sorts of trash, and carry it to a hole which he dug by the road each spring. If he was in a hurry, or the season was over and the shores were deserted, the ranger would not linger by the water but would take the buckets and go directly home. Natasha came only on Saturdays, and Olenka, who was still very little, was afraid to stay home alone.

He would walk along the springy level road between pinkish pine trunks which turned darker as they neared the ground. At their feet bilberry bushes and mushrooms poked their way through layers of gray needles.

The ranger didn't eat mushrooms; he disliked them and wouldn't pick them. Olenka gathered them, however, so for her pleasure he learned to pickle them, and after drying them in the attic, would give them to Natasha when she came.

Olenka was the ranger's niece, the daughter of his brother, a chauffeur who had died three years ago. Both the ranger, Timofey Fyodorovich, and his brother Nikolai were natives of this region. Timofey had returned from the war with one arm and had taken a job as a ranger. Nikolai had not been old enough to fight. Timofey had remained a bachelor, and Nikolai had married Natasha in 1948. A daughter was born to them and they lived together peacefully until Nikolai was killed in an accident. Before Nikolai's death, the ranger had rarely seen his brother and his family; but a year following his death, when he happened to be in the city, he stopped in to see Natasha and invited her and her daughter to visit him in the forest. He knew that Natasha, a hospital nurse, had little money.

Every summer thereafter Natasha brought Olenka to her Uncle Timofey's for a month or more, while she herself visited on Saturdays. She would tidy up the house, sweep and wash the floor, and try to be generally useful because Timofey, of course, would not accept money for Olenka. Instead of resting,

Natasha would bustle around the house, doing chores; this both angered and touched Timofey.

It was the end of August, the weather was growing unpleasant and the night air was cold and damp. The tourists were gone. It was the last Saturday of the summer season, and Timofey had promised to deliver Olenka to school in three days, for it was time for her to enter first grade. It was the last night that Natasha would sleep in Timofey's house until spring. Perhaps the ranger would come to Kalyazin for the November holidays; perhaps he would not see them again until New Year's.

Natasha was washing dishes in the river. A piece of soap lay on the sand. She washed the cups and dishes that had accumulated from dinner and supper, passed a dishcloth over the soap and rubbed the dishes with it while standing ankle-deep in the water. Then she rinsed each cup. Olenka was chilled and had run off somewhere into the bushes to look for mushrooms. The ranger sat on a rock with his jacket draped over his shoulders. They were both silent.

As she rinsed the cups, Natasha bent over, and the ranger saw her still-very-young, strong tanned legs, and he felt uneasy because he couldn't muster the courage to ask Natasha to stay on with him permanently. How simple it would have been for him if Nikolai had never existed. So he tried to look past Natasha, to the dismal gray water, to the dark wall of forest on the island, and to the solitary glow of a campfire on the opposite shore. Local fishermen, not tourists, had built the fire.

That evening Natasha, too, felt uneasy, expectant. When the ranger's glance fell on her again, she straightened up and tucked a lock of her straight auburn hair beneath her white, red-polka-dotted kerchief. Over the summer her hair, bleached by the sun, had become lighter than her skin, and her suntan made her teeth and the whites of her eyes seem even whiter. Timofey turned his glance away—Natasha, he thought, was looking at him too openly, which he felt was wrong, because he was ugly, because he was a cripple, because he was the elder brother of her deceased husband. And because he wanted her to remain here.

Natasha stood there, looking at him. Even with his eyes averted, he could not help seeing her. She had a small bosom, slender waist, and long neck. But her legs were sturdy, her hands strong. Her eyes shone in the dusk; the whites seemed brilliant. Inadvertently, Timofey met her glance, and a sweet pain coursed from his shoulder through his chest and welled in his throat in anticipation of what could and must happen today. He could not tear his eyes from Natasha. And when her lips began to move he became frightened by the words taking shape and the sound of her voice: "Tim, go home. Take Olenka —she's frozen. I'll be back soon."

Timofey rose at once, relieved and grateful to Natasha for finding the right words, kind words, meaningless though they were.

He called Olenka and went home. Natasha stayed to finish the dishes.

Dag settled down more comfortably in the shabby chair, placed the list on the table and read it aloud, marking off the lines with his fingernail. He squinted slightly—his vision was beginning to fail although he himself wasn't conscious of it or, rather, he blocked out the possibility.

"Did you take a spare transceiver?"

"I did," replied Pavlysh.

"Did you take an extra tent?"

"Here, read it first. . . . Sato, do you have any black thread?"

"No, all gone."

"You should take a third tent," said Dag.

"Unnecessary."

"Take an extra generator."

"It's on the list. Number twenty-two."

"Right. How many cylinders of compressed air are you taking?"

"Enough."

"Condensed milk? Tooth paste?"

"Man, are you getting me ready for a camping trip?"

"Take the compote. We'll manage without it."

"When I want it I'll drop in to see you."

"That won't be so easy."

"I'm only kidding," said Pavlysh. "I've no intention."

"Do as you please," said Dag.

He looked at the screen. The robots were crawling along the cables like plant lice on grass.

"Are you moving over there today?" asked Dag.

Dag was in a hurry to get home. They had already lost two days preparing their booty for transport back to Earth. And they must count on another two weeks for deceleration and maneuvering.

Sato entered the control room and announced that the launch was ready and loaded.

"According to the list?" asked Dag.

"Right. Pavlysh gave me a copy."

"Very good," said Dag. "Add a third tent."

"I already have," said Sato. "We have spare tents, but we won't need them."

"If I were you I'd move over there right now," said Dag.

"I'm ready," said Pavlysh. Dag was right. It would be better to move over there at once; then, in case anything had been overlooked, it would not be difficult to catch up with their ship and get whatever had been forgotten. He would have to spend several weeks aboard a dead spaceship that had lost its bearings and been abandoned by its occupants at some unknown time for some unknown reason. Had they not sighted the ship coursing aimlessly through space like the *Flying Dutchman,* it would have continued wandering through the black emptiness of space until pulled into orbit by some star or planet or until a collision with a meteor smashed it to smithereens.

The sector of the Galaxy through which they were returning was deserted; it lay off the beaten path and ships rarely ventured there. It was a unique, almost incredible find: an unpiloted ship, abandoned by its crew but still intact.

6

Dag calculated that if they took their trophy in tow, they would have sufficient fuel to reach the outermost bases. That is, if they jettisoned their load, casting into the emptiness of space almost everything their hard labor had won during these past twenty-two months, a labor for which all these months they had denied themselves the sight of another human face, except for their fellow crew members.

Someone had to board the trophy, maintain radio contact, and see that the ship didn't act up. That someone was Pavlysh.

"I'm on my way," said Pavlysh. "I'll set up the tent and test the transceiver."

"For God's sake, be careful," said Dag in a sudden display of emotion. "If anything—"

"Just don't lose her," replied Pavlysh. He took a last look at his cabin to see if he had forgotten anything.

Sato maneuvered the launch neatly to the dead ship's cargo hatch. Clearly a rescue launch had once stood there. Now it was gone. There was only some sort of mechanical device looming to one side.

Pushing the bundle of tents and air cylinders ahead of him, Pavlysh walked through a wide corridor toward a cabin adjoining the control room. He decided to settle down there. Judging from the room's shape and dimensions, its inhabitants were somewhat shorter than people, conceivably more massive. Had there been furniture in the cabin, it might have been possible to reconstruct an image of the ship's occupants. Perhaps this room was not a cabin but a storage compartment. They hadn't had time to inspect the ship properly. That was Pavlysh's job now. It was a huge ship; a journey through it would be anything but dull.

A camp had to be set up. Sato helped erect the tent. They installed a connecting chamber by the door and checked to see whether the tent was filling with air quickly enough. Everything was in order. Now Pavlysh had quarters where he could live without a space suit, but the suit would be needed for his walks through the ship. While he was unpacking his things in the cabin, Sato hooked up lighting and tested the transceiver. One would have thought that Sato himself was planning to stay on here, but, once finished with his work, he rejoined Dag.

They accelerated for about six hours. Dag was concerned about the strength of the towline. When they stopped accelerating, Pavlysh went to the control room and watched the jettisoned silver cylinders, flying alongside, gradually dropping behind like friends on a railroad platform. The G-forces were now tolerable, so he decided to get to work.

The control panel provided very little information. But what a strange spectacle it presented. So did the whole room. A vandal had been here. No, not an ordinary vandal, but a juvenile ham operator who had been given an expensive, complex piece of equipment to dismember. Using transistors as nails, he had converted the equipment into a crystal set, turned the printed circuit boards into props, and plastered platinum foil, like wallpaper, around his little den. Presumably—and Dag had expressed this thought the first time they had been here—the ship's operation had once been fully automated. Later someone, without any ceremony, had ripped off the panel's cover and casing, joined wires which should not be connected, and tried his damnedest to convert a chronometer into a primitive alarm clock. This vivisection had left behind a trail of excess screws, at times of inspiring proportions. The imp had scattered them all over the floor as though pressed to complete the demolition and hide before his parents returned.

Surprisingly, the room contained nothing that resembled a chair. It was possible that the ship's occupants did not know what a chair was. Perhaps they sat on the floor. Or rolled about. Pavlysh dragged his camera along and tried to photograph everything possible—just in case. If anything happened, at least they would have the film. Except for the barely audible hum of his helmet lamp, it was deathly quiet, so quiet that Pavlysh imagined he heard footsteps and shuffling noises. He was about to disconnect his interphone headset, but thought better of it; should a noise, a sound, a voice, break the silence, he would want to hear it.

The thought of such an improbable event was disquieting.

Pavlysh caught himself making an absurd gesture: he had placed his palm on the handle of his blaster.

"Atavism," he said, unaware that he had spoken aloud.

Dag's voice came through the interphone.

"What's up?"

"I keep forgetting that you're not around. It's strange here."

Pavlysh regarded himself with detachment, a little man in a shiny space suit, a tiny bug in an enormous hay-filled jar.

The corridor leading past his cabin ended as an empty, circular room. Pushing off from the hatch, he crossed it in two leaps. Beyond it began another corridor. All its walls were pale blue, slightly whitish, as if bleached by the sun. The light from his helmet lamp, spreading into a broad beam, was reflected by the walls. Ahead the corridor curved upward. Pavlysh noted it on his sketch of the ship's layout. So far the sketch suggested that the ship had an elliptical shape; the forward section of the ellipse contained a cargo hold and a hangar for a launch and rescue rocket, a control panel, a corridor connecting the panel with the circular room, and three more corridors branching from the control console. Although the location of the engine room was known, it hadn't yet been noted on the sketch. Plenty of time remained for a leisurely inspection.

About one hundred paces ahead, the corridor led to a partly opened hatch. Something white and flat lay by it. Pavlysh approached the object slowly, tilting his head to cast more light on it. It was only a rag, a white rag, brittle in the vacuum. Lifting his foot to step across it, he brushed it accidentally and the rag crumbled to dust.

"Too bad," he said.

"What happened?" asked Dag.

"Mind your own business," said Pavlysh, "or I'll disconnect."

"Just try it. I'm coming after you right now. Don't forget to sketch in the layout."

"I haven't forgotten," said Pavlysh, making a note of the hatch on the plan.

Beyond the hatch the corridor widened and branched out.

9

He selected the main one, the widest, to follow. It led to another hatch, tightly sealed.

"That's it for today," announced Pavlysh.

Dag said nothing.

"Why so silent?" asked Pavlysh.

"I'm not stopping you from talking to yourself."

"Thanks. I've reached a sealed hatch."

"Don't be in any hurry to open it."

Pavlysh lit up the wall around the hatch. He noticed a square embossment on the wall and ran his glove over it.

Suddenly Pavlysh felt that someone was standing behind him. He swung around, throwing a beam of light along the corridor. It was deserted. His nerves were on edge. He said nothing to Dag and stepped across the threshold.

Pavlysh found himself in a spacious room lined with shelves; boxes rested on several of them. He glanced into one box, but it was impossible to say what it had once contained; dust filled a third of it.

His lamp picked up another white rag in a far corner of the room, but he decided to stay clear of it until he could fix it with a preservative. When they returned to Earth it would be interesting to analyze. He focused the beam on the rag, however, and thought he saw something written on it. Perhaps he was mistaken. He took a step closer. A black inscription was clearly visible. Pavlysh bent over, then squatted.

"My name is Natasha," read the Russian letters on the cloth.

Pavlysh lost his balance and his hand touched the rag. It crumbled into dust. And with it the sign.

"My name is Natasha," repeated Pavlysh.

"What?" asked Dag.

"It said here: 'My name is Natasha.' "

"Where?"

"Nowhere now. I touched it and it vanished."

"Slava," said Dag softly. "Relax!"

"I'm completely relaxed," said Pavlysh.

Until that moment the ship had been no more than a phantom to Pavlysh, its reality merely a convention imposed, as it were, by the rules of the game. Even as he sketched in the network of corridors and hatches on the plan, he could not shake this artificially imposed perception of reality. He was like a clever mouse in a laboratory maze, but unlike a real mouse Pavlysh knew that the maze was finite and moving in cosmic space toward the solar system.

The rules had been broken by the note that had crumbled to dust. There was no possible way such a note could have gotten here; therefore only one rational conclusion could be drawn: it had never existed. That's precisely what Dag had concluded. In his place, Pavlysh would have agreed, but Pavlysh could not change places with Dag.

"Did you say 'Natasha'?" asked Dag.

"Yes, 'Natasha.' "

"Listen, Slava. You're a physiologist. You know what I'm trying to say. Maybe we should replace you? Or forget about inspecting the ship?"

"Everything is OK. Don't worry. I just went back for some fixative."

"What for?"

"If I come across another note, I'll save it for you."

While rummaging through a box of assorted objects packed by the efficient Sato, Pavlysh tried to visualize the rag or piece of paper with its inscription, but it eluded him. By the time he returned to the chamber where the small heap of white dust greeted him, his confidence in the note's existence was shaken.

"What are you doing?" asked Dag.

"Looking for a hatch, so I can go further."

"How was it written?"

"In Russian."

"What kind of writing? What sort of letters?"

"Letters? Printed. Large ones."

He found a hatch. It opened easily into strange-looking quarters partitioned into compartments of various sizes and shapes.

Some were enclosed in glass, others were separated from the corridor by fine screening. In the middle of the corridor stood a hemisphere, some two feet in diameter, that resembled a huge tortoise. Pavlysh touched it, and with surprising ease the object rolled through the corridor as if propelled by concealed, well-oiled rollers. It collided with the wall and stopped dead. His helmet lamp picked out nooks and recesses in the darkness. But all were empty. In one pile lay stones; in another, wood scraps. On closer observation the scraps turned out to be the remains of some large insect. Pavlysh advanced slowly, constantly keeping the ship informed of his progress.

"You've got quite a thing there," came Dag's voice. "I bet that ship was abandoned about forty years ago."

"Maybe thirty?"

"Maybe even fifty. The Brain gave us a preliminary report."

"Don't knock yourself out," said Pavlysh. "Even thirty years ago we still hadn't ventured beyond the solar system."

"I know. But I'll verify the Brain's report. As long as you're not hallucinating."

There was nothing to verify. Particularly since they knew that the ship they had found was not coming from the Sun. In any case, it had been traveling toward the Sun for many years and would have had to spend many years to get that far away in the first place. It was only forty or fifty years since people had pioneered Mars and landed on Pluto. Beyond Pluto lay space as mysterious as the lands beyond the ocean had been to the ancients. And no one in this sector of space could speak or write Russian—

Pavlysh climbed to the next level and tried to find his way through a maze of corridors, recesses, and chambers. After half an hour he said: "They were junk collectors."

"What about Natasha?"

"Nothing more on her yet."

Could he have missed traces of Natasha, walked right by them? Even on Earth, when one withdraws from the everyday world of airports and large cities, one loses the ability, as well as the right, to judge the real meaning of the things and

12

phenomena one encounters. How much more true this was for the objects on an alien spaceship: the hemisphere, rolling away so easily from his feet; the recesses with their forgotten objects, and tools whose functions were a mystery; the tangled maze of wires and pipes; the bright stains on the walls; the bars on the ceiling; the sections of slippery floor; and the ruptured, semitransparent membranes. What sort of creatures had controlled the ship? Here, for example, was a room which giants must have inhabited; another which must have been designed for gnomes; out there was a frozen swimming pool with what looked like oblong bodies frozen in its turbid ice. Then he entered a spacious room whose entire wall was covered by a machine studded with blank screens, and rows of knobs from the floor up reached some fifteen feet above his head.

The total absence of logic and consistency in what he observed around him was frustrating. It prevented him from constructing even a loose working hypothesis or threading one with facts, which was precisely what his brain, exhausted from stumbling through this maze, demanded.

Behind the widely spaced bars lay a black mass that had shriveled in the vacuum. It was most likely the remains of a creature about the size of an elephant. Perhaps it had been one of the astronauts. But the cell-like structure had cut him off from the corridor. Why would he have hidden behind those bars? A rather ugly explanation occurred to him: the astronaut had been confined to a cell as punishment. Yes, this must have been the ship's brig. And when an emergency forced the crew to abandon ship in great haste, the prisoner had been forgotten. Or deliberately left behind.

Pavlysh repeated his thoughts to Dag.

Dag didn't agree with him. "That emergency launch had a very small capacity. You saw the size of the hangar."

Dag was right.

On the floor beside the dark mass lay an empty circular vessel about twenty inches in diameter.

About thirty minutes later, behind a closed but unlocked hatch in the next corridor, Pavlysh found the compartment

13

where Natasha had lived. Halting on the threshold, he looked at the bunk, neatly covered with a gray spread; at the washed-out, threadbare, red polka-dotted kerchief on the floor; at the cup with a broken handle, sitting on a shelf. On each subsequent trip to the room he noticed more of Natasha's belongings and found traces of her presence elsewhere on the ship. But it was the red polka dots on the kerchief and the cup with the broken handle that made a deep impression on him the first time he saw her quarters. The presence of these two objects was far more incredible than any strange machine or device he would ever encounter.

"OK, here," announced Pavlysh. Hoping to preserve everything in the cabin as it appeared the instant he had discovered it, he pressed the button on the can of fixative.

"What are you jabbering about?" asked Dag.

"I found Natasha."

"You what!"

"Well, not Natasha herself, but where she lived."

"Are you serious?"

"Dead serious. Her cup is here. She also forgot her kerchief."

"Listen," said Dag, "I know you haven't gone bananas. But I still can't believe it."

"Neither can I."

"Can you picture this?" said Dag. "We've landed on the moon and see a girl sitting there, sitting and embroidering, for example."

"Sounds just as wild," Pavlysh agreed. "But that's her cup over there. With a broken handle."

"But where's Natasha?" asked Sato.

"I don't know," said Pavlysh. "She hasn't been here for a long time."

"OK, what else?" asked Dag. "Tell me something about her. What was she like?"

"She was pretty," said Sato.

"Naturally," Pavlysh agreed. "Very pretty."

Behind the bunk a small box filled with objects caught his

eye. It appeared that Natasha had been preparing to go somewhere but something had forced her to abandon her belongings and leave empty-handed.

Pavlysh sprayed the objects with fixative and stored them on the bunk: a skirt sewn from plastic with thick nylon thread; a sack with slits for head and arms; a shawl, or cape, woven from colored wires.

"She lived here a long time," said Pavlysh.

At the very bottom of the box lay a sheaf of square white sheets covered with an even script which slanted heavily to the right. Pavlysh restrained himself from reading them until he could fix them with preservative to make absolutely certain that they would not crumble beneath his fingers.

"Read them aloud," asked Dag, but Pavlysh refused. He was very tired. But he promised to read the most interesting parts to him after he had looked through the material himself. Dag didn't argue with him.

I found this paper two months ago but couldn't find anything to write with. Yesterday, I finally realized that there was a pile of stones, similar to graphite, in the next room, which was guarded by a *gloopy.** I sharpened one of them. So now I shall write. [The following day Pavlysh discovered long columns of scratches on the wall of Natasha's cabin and guessed that she had kept track of the days.]

I have been wanting for so long to keep a diary because I hope that some day, though I may not live to see that bright moment, someone will find me. One cannot live without at least some hope. At times I regret that I am an atheist. If I believed, I could put my faith in God and comfort myself with the thought that all my suffering is a test from above.

With this the page ended. Pavlysh realized that Natasha did not make daily entries in her diary, although the pages were piled in order. Sometimes weeks would pass before she resumed her entries.

*"gloopy"—in Russian *glupyi* means stupid

15

They are bustling about today. It's gotten worse. I'm coughing again. The air here is deadly. I suppose people can learn to adjust to anything. Even to captivity. But there is nothing worse than being alone. I've learned to talk aloud to myself. At first I felt awkward and embarrassed, as though someone might be listening. Now I even sing aloud. I must put down how all this came about in case, God forbid, anyone else finds himself in this situation. Today I feel very poorly. On the way to the kitchen garden I was so breathless I slumped down right by the wall and the gloopies dragged me back half dead.

Several days later Pavlysh found Natasha's kitchen garden.

I am writing now because I can't go anywhere, anyway. The gloopies won't let me. I suppose we must wait for an addition to our family. But I don't know whether I'll see—

The third page was written in a finer and neater hand. Natasha was trying to conserve paper.

Should anyone ever chance to come here, they should know the following about me. My name is Natasha Matveevna Sidorova. I was born in 1923 in the village of Gorodishche, Yaroslavl Oblast. I completed high school in the village and was preparing to enter the institute when my father died, and it was very difficult for Mother to work alone on the collective farm and manage the household. So I began to work on the farm, although I never lost hope of continuing my education. When my sisters Vera and Valentina got a little older, I fulfilled my dream and entered the nursing institute in Yaroslavl and graduated in 1942. I was drafted into the army and spent the war years as a nurse in military hospitals. After the war I returned to Gorodishche and accepted a nursing position at a local hospital. I married in 1948. We moved to Kalyazin, and the following year I gave birth to a daughter, Olenka. My husband, Nikolai Ivanov, a chauffeur, died in 1953 as the result of an accident. So Olenka and I remained all alone.

Pavlysh, inside the white tent, sat on the floor in a corner of the room reading Natasha's autobiography aloud. Her handwriting was easy to read; she wrote neatly, her letters were well rounded and slanted to the right. Here and there the graphite had crumbled, so Pavlysh had to tilt the page to make out the letters. He put aside the page and picked up the next one, expecting to find her story continued.

"So in 1953 she was thirty years old," said Sato.

"Keep reading," said Dag.

"She writes here about something else," said Pavlysh. "I'll read it to you in a minute."

"Read it now." Dag was annoyed.

They dragged in new captives today. They locked them up in empty cages on the lower floor. I couldn't see how many were brought in. But I think there were several. A gloopy closed their door and wouldn't let me in to see them. I suddenly realized how much I envied them. Yes, I envied these unfortunates, torn forever from their homes and families and imprisoned for crimes they never committed. Envied them because there were many of them. Perhaps three, maybe five. But they were together, and I was completely alone. Time here is always the same. If I were not used to working, I would have died long ago. How many years have I been here? More than four, I think. I must check it, count the scratches on the wall. But I think I may have lost count. Well, I must get back to work. A gloopy brought me some thread and wire. They do appear to understand something. I found a needle on the third floor, although a gloopy did want to take it away from me. Poor thing, it was frightened.

"Well?" asked Dag.

"I won't be able to read everything," replied Pavlysh. "Hold on. Here's something that looks like a continuation."

Later I'll put these pages in order. I keep thinking that someone will read them. I won't be alive; my remains will be scattered among the stars, but these scraps of paper will survive. I beg whoever reads this, please try to find my little daughter Olenka. Perhaps she's grown up by now. Tell her what happened to her mother. Although she will never find my grave, I will feel easier knowing she will be aware of my fate. If anyone had ever told me that I would be locked up in a terrible prison and would go on living while everyone believed me dead, I would have died of fright. Yet I am living. Oh, how I hope that Timofey won't think that I left my little girl on his hands and ran off to seek the easy life. No, I suppose he won't; most likely they searched the entire channel and concluded that I had drowned. That day will remain etched in my memory until the end of my days because it was so extraordinary. Not because of the terrible calamity that befell me. On the contrary. Because on that day something in my life was about to change for the better. But it certainly didn't turn out that way.

"No," said Pavlysh, putting aside the page. "It's too personal."

"What's too personal?"

"Here—about Timofey. Some friend of hers. Maybe from the hospital. Hold on, let me look ahead."

"Who the hell are you to decide what's to be read!" shouted Dag. "You're in such a damned hurry, you'll skip something important."

"Calm down. I won't miss anything important," replied Pavlysh. "These scraps of paper are very old. We can't find her and save her. You could just as well be reading a cuneiform text. Same difference."

After Nikolai's death I remained quite alone with Olenka. Of course there were my sisters. But they lived very far away and had their own families and cares. We weren't well off; I worked at the hospital and was appointed senior nurse in the spring of 1956. Olenka was supposed to start school the following fall. I had marriage proposals, including one from a doctor at our hospital, a really fine man, middle-aged. But

I refused him because I felt my youth had passed; I was content with just the two of us, Olenka and myself. Timofey Ivanov, my husband's brother, a disabled veteran who worked as a forest ranger not far from the city, helped me. I met this terrible fate at the end of August 1956. I don't remember the date, but I do remember that it happened on a Saturday evening. The situation was as follows:

We were especially busy at the hospital because many employees were taking summer vacations and I had to fill in for other staff. Fortunately, Timofey, as always, took Olenka for the summer. I went there Saturdays by bus and had a good rest if I had Sunday off, too. His house was in a pine forest near the Volga.

Pavlysh paused.
"Well, what then?" asked Dag.
"Hold on. I'm looking for the next page."

I shall try to describe in detail what happened, because as a medical worker I understand the importance of a correct diagnosis, and to make one, someone will need all the details. If my description falls into the hands of an expert, perhaps it will help him solve similar cases should they occur.

That evening Timofey and Olenka had accompanied me to the river to wash dishes. The road leading from the house to the Volga goes right to the water's edge. Timofey wanted to wait for me but I was afraid that Olenka would catch cold because it was a cool evening; so I asked him to go back and told him I would return soon. It wasn't quite dark yet, and about two or three minutes after my dear ones had started back, I heard a low, buzzing noise. At first I wasn't afraid because I thought it was a motorboat some distance away on the Volga. Then, quite suddenly, I had a strange feeling of impending disaster. I looked at the river but didn't see any motorboat—

Pavlysh found the next page.

Flying toward me, barely above my head, I saw an airship that looked like a submarine without fins. It looked silvery. The ship landed directly in front of me, cutting me off from the road. I was amazed. During the war I had seen all sorts of military equipment, so at first I thought this was a new type of aircraft making a forced landing because its engine had failed. I wanted to run away from it, to hide behind a pine tree in case it should explode. But the craft released iron claws and out of them fell the gloopies. I didn't know then what these gloopies were. At that instant everything grew hazy and I probably fainted.

"Then what?" asked Dag, when Pavlysh's silence grew prolonged.
"Then nothing."
"So what happened?"
"She doesn't say anything else about that."
"Well, what does she have to say?"
Pavlysh remained silent, reading to himself.

I know the way to the lower level. A path leads from the kitchen garden, and the gloopies leave it unguarded. I was very anxious to see the new arrivals. But all my neighbors were lower creatures. So I learned to visit the dragon in its cage. At first I was afraid. But once I happened to see what the gloopies fed it: grasses from the kitchen garden. Then I realized that it wouldn't eat me. Perhaps I would have waited much longer before I began to visit the dragon, but one day as I was passing its cage, I noticed that it was ill. The gloopies were fussing over it, offering food, and taking measurements. It lay on its side, breathing heavily. I went up to the bars and looked at it closely. After all, I am a nurse, and it is my duty to relieve suffering. I could not help the gloopies if they were ill; they were made of iron. But I did manage to examine the dragon through the bars. It was injured. Probably, it had tried to break out of the cage and had bruised itself against the bars. God had endowed it generously with brawn, but not with brain. I felt a terrible sense of despair; life was so cheap. I thought to myself: it's used to me. It arrived here before me and has seen me thousands of times. I told the gloopies not to interfere with me, and to bring some warm water. Of course, I was taking a chance. Laboratory tests were out of the question. But its wounds were beginning to fester, so I cleaned and bandaged them as best as I could. The dragon did not resist and even turned around to make it easier for me.

Apparently the next page had come from the bottom of the pile; it did not logically follow the preceding page.

I sat down to write today, but my hands would not obey me. A bird had escaped from its cage, so the gloopies chased it down the corridor with a net. I wanted to catch it, too, fearing it might injure itself badly. My efforts were in vain. It flew into the large hall, struck a pipe in flight, and fell. Later, when the gloopies were dragging it to the museum, I picked up a feather, long and thin like feather-grass. I felt sorry for the bird, but envied it, too. Having failed to make a break to freedom, it had found the courage to die. A year ago such an example could have had a decisive influence on me. But now I am busy; I cannot waste my life for nothing. As unrealistic as my goal may be, it is there. So in this disturbed and contemplative mood, I followed the gloopies to the museum. They forgot to close the door behind them. I did not enter —it hasn't any air—but I looked through the glass wall. I saw jars, stills, vessels, where the gloopies preserved in formaldehyde or a similar fluid those creatures that did not survive the journey. Like freaks in Leningrad's Cabinet of Curiosities. I realized that in a few more years my corpse, too, would be neither cremated nor buried, but placed in a glass jar for the gloopies and their masters to admire. How pained I was. I told Bal about it; he shivered, implying that he feared the same fate. As I sit here writing these lines, I picture myself in a glass jar, preserved in alcohol

Several days later Pavlysh found the museum. Space's low temperature had frozen the liquid in which the exhibits had been preserved. Pavlysh passed slowly from vessel to vessel, peering carefully into the ice of the larger jars. He was afraid of finding Natasha's body. Dag's and Sato's impatient demands for information rang in his ears. Pavlysh shared Natasha's fears. Any fate would be preferable to a jar of formaldehyde. He did find the jar with the bird, an iridescent, ephemeral creature with a long tail, a large eye, and a head without a beak. He also found a jar containing Bal; an account of him appeared in the pages that followed.

I keep digressing from my story because today's events are more important than what happened in the years gone by. Therefore, I find it impossible to describe my experiences in order.

I regained consciousness in a tiny, dimly lit room. Not the room where I now live. That tiny room is now strewn with fossilized cockleshells dragged in by the gloopies about a year ago. In a little more than four years we have stopped sixteen times, and each time there was a great deal of excitement as all sorts of objects, including living creatures, were hauled in here. So, for example, besides myself in that tiny room, were the dishes I had been washing when I was seized, pine branches, grass, stones, and various insects. Only later did I realize that they were trying to find out how to feed me. At that time I didn't realize that those objects had been placed there deliberately. I didn't eat; I had more important things to think about. I sat down, tapped along the wall—it was hard, and I kept hearing a whirring noise all around me, like the engines of an ocean liner. Also, I had a sensation of extreme lightness. Generally everything is lighter here than on Earth. I had read once that the pull of gravity on the moon was also less, and if someday, as Tsiolkovsky predicted, people fly to the stars, they will weigh nothing at all. It was this reduced gravitational pull that told me very soon that I was no longer on Earth, that I had been kidnapped, spirited away, and that my captors were unable to transport me to their destination. I sincerely hope that people, ours on Earth, will learn to travel in space someday. But I fear that day is a long way off.

Pavlysh had read those lines aloud. Dag said, "And to think she died only a year before Sputnik."
Sato corrected him. "She was alive when Gagarin made his flight."
"Maybe. But it wasn't any comfort to her."
"It would have been, if she had known about it," said Pavlysh.
"I'm not so sure," said Dag. "Then she would have expected to be rescued. And would have waited in vain."
"That's not the point," said Pavlysh. "It would have meant a lot to her to know that we had learned to travel in space."
He continued to read aloud until he grew tired.

They brought me something to eat and stood in the doorway watching to see if I would taste it. I tried it, a strange-tasting gruel, slightly salty. A most unappetizing meal. But I was hungry then and still in a daze. I kept looking at the gloopies, standing there like tortoises, and asked them to summon their chief. I didn't know at the time that their chief was the Machine, a device that occupied the entire wall of a distant room. And I still know nothing about the real masters of this ship, manned only by robots. I wondered then how they figured out what kind of food would not harm me. I racked my brains until I saw the laboratory and surmised that they had drawn some blood from me while I was unconscious and had studied my body thoroughly. They understood what I needed and in what proportions, so that I wouldn't die of starvation. But they haven't any notion of what is tasty. My anger at the gloopies has long since subsided. Like soldiers, they are only carrying out orders. Except soldiers are capable of thought. The gloopies aren't. During my first days in captivity I cried continuously, begging in vain for my freedom—

Suddenly I've begun to feel strangely uneasy. Probably because I'm no longer alone. I've a feeling that there's going to be a change soon. I don't know yet if it will be for the better. But things can't get worse. Today I dreamed of Olenka, and in my dream I was surprised that she hadn't grown, that she was still running about as a little girl. It's time she had grown up. But she only laughed. When I woke up I was very alarmed. Did this mean that Olenka was no longer in the world? I was never one to believe in premonitions. But later it occurred to me that I had no way of knowing whether I had kept proper track of time. Hadn't I been scratching off the days when I awoke each morning? But suppose it wasn't morning? Maybe I was sleeping more now? Or less? How would I know? Time is always the same here. Then I thought that perhaps two years, not four, had passed. Or maybe one? Or even five, six, or seven years? How old would Olenka be now? And I? Maybe I'm already an old woman? I became so agitated that I ran to the mirrors. Not real ones, of course. They were convex and circular, somewhat like television screens. Sometimes green and blue lines zigzagged across them. I had no other mirror. I stared at my reflection for a long time. Even the gloopies who were on duty there began to signal to me, asking what I needed. I simply waved them away. The time had passed when I thought of them as executioners, torturers, and Fascists. I no longer fear them. I fear only the Machine. The Chief. I studied myself in the mirrors for a long time, going from one to the other, looking for the brightest one. I could not decide anything. It was like me: same nose, eyes sunken, and my face had a bluish cast. Most likely from the mirror. Of course, bags under my eyes. I returned to my room.

"Extremely interesting," said Dag. "What do you think, Pavlysh?"
"About what?"
"About this problem. Isolate a person for several years so

that he is unaware of the passage of time outside. Will his biological clock change?"

"I'm thinking about something else at the moment."

I suddenly remembered the kitten. I had completely forgotten her. Today I remembered. A kitten had been brought aboard from somewhere. From Earth, of course. She whined and meowed. That was the first few days. She whined in the little room next to mine, and the gloopies kept running to her, absolutely unable to figure out that she needed milk. I was very timid then, and they took me to the kitten, thinking I could help her. But I could not get them to understand what milk was. It was obvious that something was lacking in their synthetic food. I fussed over the kitten for three days. I diluted cereal with water. In my concern for the kitten, I forgot about my own troubles. But the kitten died. It's clear that people can endure more than animals, although it's said a cat has nine lives. But I am still alive. The kitten is probably in the museum's collection. Now I could find the proper synthetic diet for her because I know the way to the laboratory. And the gloopies' attitude toward me has changed. They're used to me. But the dragon is doing very poorly. It will die soon. I sat with it a long time yesterday and cleansed its wounds again. It has grown much weaker. I've made an amazing discovery: it seems that the dragon, in some unknown fashion, can affect my thoughts. Not that I understand the dragon, but when it's in pain, I can sense it. I know it's glad to see me. Now I'm sorry that I hadn't paid attention to it before; but I was afraid. Who knows; it might even be a prisoner like me. But more unfortunate. All these years it has been locked up in a cage. Maybe this dragon was a nurse in a hospital on some remote planet. And, like myself, she had come to see her little daughter and had fallen into the clutches of this zoo. And spent many years here behind bars. And kept trying to get the gloopies to understand that she was not more stupid than they. But she'll die without having communicated with them. At first when I thought about it, I laughed; then I cried. Here I am now, sitting and weeping, and I must go, for they are waiting for me.

Still, when I think about the dragon, I feel my fate is better. At least I have a certain measure of freedom and have had it from the very beginning. Since the kitten died, I've often wondered why all the other captives are locked up. I alone am permitted to wander freely among the decks. For some reason they decided that I presented no danger to them. Perhaps their masters resemble me. They entrusted the kitten to me. They allowed me into the kitchen garden and showed me where the seeds were. I also have access to the laboratory. Even the gloopies obey me. Whoever reads these pages will undoubtedly wonder what these gloopies are. I call them iron tortoises. As soon as I realized they were machines and didn't understand simple things, I began to call them gloopies. To myself. Still, when you think about it, I'm not much better off than those creatures behind bars. Or those locked up in tiny rooms. The only advantage is that my prison is roomier than theirs. And that's the sum total of it. Through the gloopies, I tried to explain to the Machine, the mastermind, that it was downright criminal to kidnap a person and detain her like this. I wanted to explain that it would be better for them to establish contact with us, with Earth. But later I became convinced that there was no one here—only machines. The machines had been ordered to fly through the universe, collect everything in their path, and then report their findings to their home base. But the return flight is a very long one. I still hope I shall survive it; and if I do, I shall meet them and tell them everything. Perhaps they are unaware of the existence of intelligent life outside their own planet.

When Pavlysh finished reading the page aloud, Dag said:
"I would say that her reasoning, on the whole, was quite logical."
"Of course the ship was a research robot," said Pavlysh.

"But there is one puzzling element here. And Natasha picked it up."

"What's that?" asked Sato.

"I think it's very strange that such an enormous ship, sent on such a distant mission, had no contact whatsoever with a base, with its own planet. Obviously it had been cruising for many years. And information becomes obsolete."

"I disagree," said Dag. "Suppose there are several such ships. Each is assigned to a sector of the Galaxy. And let's assume they cruise for many years. It makes no difference. They find, God forbid, organic life on one in a thousand worlds. So they cart off the information. What is one hundred years to a civilization capable of sending out reconnaissance craft? Later, at their leisure, they can examine their trophies and decide where to send expeditions."

"And they seize everything that crosses their path?" Sato could not conceal his hostility toward the ship's masters.

"But what criteria can robots possibly have to determine whether the creature they have snared is an intelligent one?"

"Well, Natasha, for example, was clothed. They've seen our cities."

"I can't buy that," said Pavlysh. "Who's to say that intelligent people in World X aren't nudists and don't clothe their pets?"

Dag shook his head. "But the odds against their fishing out intelligent creatures are so great, they probably overlooked them. In any case they try to take their trophies alive."

"You're wasting your breath," said Pavlysh, turning to the next page. "We still don't know anything about the parties who dispatched the ship. And we don't know what they had in mind. There's nothing like them in any part of the Galaxy explored by man. So they came from some remote corner. All we know is that they visited our planet and, for some reason, did not return home."

"Maybe it's a good thing they didn't," said Dag.

The others remained silent.

Somehow, later on, I'll find the time to write about my first few years in captivity. At the moment so much seems hazy and distant—my terror and desperation, my attempts to find a way out; I had even thought of breaking into the control room and smashing their machines. So what if we all perished? These were my thoughts when I feared they would visit Earth again and do something terrible. However, I realized that I couldn't cope with the ship's technology. Nor could a hundred engineers. But now it's time for me to return to those events which occurred rather recently, months or weeks ago, after I had found some paper and began to keep a diary.

The new prisoners picked up in the last catch were placed on my deck, probably because we required the same kind of air. At first they were quarantined on another deck and then sent to tiny rooms near my own quarters. My hopes soared: perhaps they, too, were people, or at least humanoid. But when I saw them—I noticed the gloopies bringing food to their cells—I realized that I was to be terribly disappointed again. I remember, one time, seeing trepangs for sale in a market in Yaroslavl. I wondered then how people could eat such vile stuff. Other customers in the market reacted as I had. The newly captured animals resembled those trepangs. They were about the size of a dog, slippery and repulsive-looking. I returned to my quarters so upset that I couldn't even begin to write anything about them in my diary. If my hopes hadn't been so high, I wouldn't have been so disappointed. The trepangs were not permitted to leave their quarters. Soon I learned that there were five of them—two in a tiny room and three in a cage, behind an iron door. I saw their food soon, too, because the gloopies cramped my kitchen garden, cultivating tubs full of some sort of living mold that moved and smelled bad. And they dragged these tubs of mold to the trepangs.

The dragon has taken another turn for the worse. I performed some tests in the laboratory. Ivan Akimovich, on our hospital staff, should have seen me. He always urged me to continue my studies, said that with my fine intuitive sense I'd make a good doctor. But life had drained me and I remained an ignoramus, much to my regret now. True, I substituted as a laboratory technician on many occasions, and I knew how to perform lab tests and assist at operations. A small hospital is a good training ground, and I would advise all young nurses to spend some time in one. But of what use would my knowledge be here?

"Why so silent?" asked Dag. "Skipping something?"

"You'll read it through yourself. I'm trying to get to the real stuff," replied Pavlysh.

Though the sight of the trepangs was revolting, I realized that my reaction was unfair; they hadn't done me any harm. Moreover, I was now accustomed to living among wonders and freaks that no nightmare could equal. When I count up my days here, the endless, monotonous chain they form is terrifying. But when I think about it, I realize that each day brings something new. What a hardy creature man is! Surely the other captives, and perhaps my dragon too, look upon me as a freak.

The trepangs are probably capable of thought. This occurred to me when I noticed them following me with their eyes and stirring as I passed their cage. Once when I was coming from the kitchen garden with a bunch of radishes— puny, droopy, but still a source of vitamins—a trepang was fiddling about by the bars. It looked as if it were trying to break the lock. Well, I thought, that's precisely what occurred to me when I had been locked up at the beginning, and the times when they locked me in because they were approaching other planets. I thought about it and halted for an instant. I wondered what it meant? Maybe they could think. Like me. No sooner did a trepang notice me than it hissed and slithered back, away from the bars. But not in time, because one of the gloopies was standing nearby (I was so used to ignoring them that I didn't see it) and gave the trepang an electric shock. That's how they punish us. The trepang shrank back. I shouted at the gloopy and wanted to continue on my way, but then I caught it too. The gloopy gave me such a powerful shock that I fell down and scattered the radishes. Clearly it was trying to teach me to stay away from the trepangs.

Somehow I managed to get to my feet. After all the time I've spent here I still cannot get used to the idea that I am no more to them than a guinea pig. They could kill me at any moment and I would end up in a jar in the museum's collection. And they wouldn't be punished for it. I clenched my teeth and went to my quarters.

Later it turned out that my punishment was not without its benefits. Before that, the trepangs had believed I was one of the masters; they had even assumed that I was the chief here. If not for the punishment administered to me by the gloopies, they would have continued to consider me their enemy. So, about three days later, as I was on my way to nurse the dragon again, I saw one of the trepangs fussing around by the bars and hissing. Very softly. I looked around. Not a gloopy in sight. "Having a bad time of it?" I asked. During those past few days I had grown accustomed to the trepangs and no longer looked upon them as freaks. The trepang kept hissing and making clicking sounds. Then I realized that it was trying to communicate with me. "I don't understand," I said. I was about to smile, but then thought better of it: perhaps my smile might appear more frightening than a wolf's snarling. The trepang hissed again. I said: "What are you trying to tell me? I don't have a dictionary of your language. If you're not poisonous, we'll certainly get to understand each other." It fell silent, and listened for something. A large gloopy with arms like a grasshopper suddenly appeared in the corridor. The keeper. Although I knew that such gloopies did not punish their captives with electric shocks, I hurried on my way, not wanting to be seen near the cage. But when I returned I stayed a while and chatted.

Later it occurred to me that it might be easier for them to communicate with me via the written word. So I wrote out my name on a piece of paper, brought it to the trepang, and repeated it aloud while showing it to him. I'm afraid it didn't understand.

Two days later one of the trepangs had an encounter with the gloopies. I think it had managed to open the lock and was caught in the corridor. It fell into the gloopies' hands and they knocked it around badly while they summoned others to assist them. The trepang tried to resist them. I was in the corridor, heard the commotion, and ran to the scene; but it was too late. The trepang had already been isolated in another tiny room with a new lock. The other trepangs were very upset and restless. I tried to get into the isolated trepang's room, but the gloopies wouldn't let me through. Then I decided to take a stand. I planted myself next to the door and stayed there. I waited until they opened the door and I managed to glance inside. Covered with wounds, the trepang lay on the floor. I went to the laboratory, picked up my medical kit—this was not the first time I had to render first aid—and headed for the little room. When a gloopy tried to stop me, I showed it the contents of my kit. The gloopy froze on the spot. I knew by now that this posture was assumed whenever they sought the Machine's advice. I waited. One minute passed. Suddenly the gloopy stepped to one side.

I sat with the trepang for three hours. I treated the gloopies like my own hospital orderlies. They brought me water, but I could not convince them to bring in another trepang. After all, their own kind would know better than me what the hurt one needed. Then the most astonishing thing happened the very moment the gloopies were out of the room: the trepang began to hiss again, and I could distinguish in its hissing the words, "What are you trying to do?" I realized that it had memorized my conversation with it and was trying to imitate me. For the first time in many months, I was jubilant. It was not only imitating me; it actually understood what it was doing.

The speed with which they memorized my words was startling, and they tried so hard to pronounce them, although their tube-shaped mouths and lack of teeth made it difficult. During those days and weeks I lived as in a dream. A beautiful dream. I noticed remarkable changes in myself. I believed there wasn't a more agreeable creature in the world than a trepang. I became aware of their beauty and learned to distinguish them as individuals. But I must admit in all honesty that I was absolutely unable to decipher their own hissing and clicking sounds. And I still cannot. I taught them words whenever the opportunity presented itself. I would walk past them, say a word, carry various objects next to the cage to illustrate words. And they understood at once. They learned my name, and as soon as they saw me (if the gloopies weren't around) they would hiss, "Nashasha, Nashasha!" Like little children! I learned what they liked to eat from the kitchen garden and tried to feed them from time to time, although their food had an awful odor which I simply could not get used to. The Machine had given the gloopies strict instructions about the trepangs: they must remain locked up, under constant surveillance, guarded, and not trusted. So I could not meet with them openly or I, too, would have become suspect. What was also amazing was this: until now I had not been a threat to the gloopies. Because I had been alone. But now, allied, the trepangs and I had become a force to be reckoned with. I felt this. And when the trepangs learned to speak Russian they told me they too felt the same way. So the day arrived when I went up to their cage and heard: "Natasha, we must get out of here."

"But where can you go from here?" I replied. "God knows where this ship is going. We don't even know where we are now. Besides, how could we pilot the ship?"

Trepang Bal replied: "Not yet. After we learn more about it. And you must help us."

"But how can I?"

The two of them began squealing and hissing at me, trying to persuade me. I only smiled. I couldn't tell them I was happy. Whether we succeeded or not didn't matter. What an alliance—the trepangs and I! My little Olenka ought to see her old mama now, strolling through the blue corridor past locked doors and cages, and singing "We Shall Overcome on Land and Sea!"

"So she found allies," Pavlysh replied curtly to Dag's insistent demands that he read aloud. "Listen, Dag, I can skim through these pages ten times faster if I read them to myself." Before Dag had a chance to get a word in, Pavlysh was reading the next page.

I didn't write anything for several days. No time. No, I wasn't busier than usual; it's just that my mind was too occupied with other things. I even gave myself a haircut; I stood before the dark mirrors for a long time, hacking my hair with a scalpel. I'd give my right arm for an iron. To be sure, no one sees me here; for that matter, no one except me knows what ironing is or what clothes are. How much time I've wasted trying to figure out what to use for cloth and thread so I could make myself something. Robinson Crusoe was better off than me. As I stood before the mirror, I thought I never did have occasion to dress fashionably. If I were to appear on Earth right now, everyone would probably stare at me in wonder, thinking, what kind of back number is that? According to my calculations it's 1960 on Earth now. What are women wearing now? I suppose it depends on where you are. Of course, in Moscow they're wearing the latest styles. But Kalyazin is a small city.

Oh, I've certainly digressed. Thinking about rags. Ridiculous, isn't it? Especially in the light of Bal's sacrifice. My favorite trepang deliberately injured himself so he could learn my language better. He cut himself very badly, and the gloopies summoned me for help. They already knew me as their "first aid" resource. I gave Bal a good dressing down, forgetting about his retentive memory. So now he has memorized all my nasty words. Oh, they aren't so awful: "goof," "simpleton," and the like. Since I can move about our prison freely, I have two tasks now: one, to maintain communication between the cells where the trepangs are

33

confined; two, to reconnoiter behind enemy lines and learn the location of all objectives. Yes, I remembered our wartime lessons well.

The following page, written in great haste, was very brief.

Dola had me make three trips beyond the bulkhead, to the large chamber. I told him what I had found. Dola is in charge now. Apparently the trepangs had decided among themselves that my help was not sufficient. Bal must go to the control room. I'll take him to the bulkhead. From there he'll follow the map I sketched. I'll wait for him at the bulkhead. I'm worried about Bal. The gloopies are much sharper than Bal. He'll start out now while the gloopies are busy on other decks.

The entry broke off here. The next one was in a different hand; the script was small and austere.

Something terrible has happened. I was standing behind the bulkhead, waiting for Bal and counting to myself. I thought that if he returned before I reached one thousand, everything would be all right. But he didn't. He was delayed. Signals flashed and hummed, as usually happens when something is wrong on the ship. Gloopies rushed past me. I tried to shut the door to keep them out, but one gave me an electric shock that almost knocked me unconscious. They killed Bal. He's in the museum now. I had to hide in my room until everything quieted down. I was afraid they would lock me up, but for some reason they did not take me seriously.

About two hours later, when I went into the corridor and trudged toward my kitchen garden—it was time to give my dragon its vitamins—I found gloopies standing by the trepangs' cage door. I had to pass without glancing in their direction. I didn't know then that Bal had been killed. It wasn't until evening that I managed to exchange a few words with the trepangs. Dola told me about Bal's death. I was very upset that night; I remembered what a dear, affectionate, beautiful creature Bal had been. I wasn't pretending. I was

34

sincerely disturbed. I also thought all was lost now, that no one else would manage to get into the control room. But Dola told me today that there still was hope. It appeared that the trepangs were capable of communicating and conversing out of sight of each other, even at great distances, by means of some brain wave phenomenon. And so Bal had lingered in order to transmit to his comrades the entire layout of the ship's control room and his thoughts about it. He had even approached the Machine itself. He knew that he would probably die, but he felt that he must transmit all the information to us. The Machine did kill him. Well, maybe not the Machine itself. After all, it's only a machine. But that's how it turned out.

I wondered what my great grandfathers had thought and felt about the world around them. They were illiterate serfs. They believed the Earth to be the center of the universe. They knew nothing of Giordano Bruno or Copernicus. Imagine if they were here now. But what difference is there, really, between them and myself? Although I had read in the newspapers about the infinite universe, it never had an effect on my life. I still lived in the center of the universe—my house on Zimmermanova Street in Kalyazin. It seems that my world was a remote, godforsaken place . . .

Dag said something to Pavlysh, who mumbled a few incoherent words, like someone awakened from a sound sleep.

For the first time in all these years I was awakened by the cold. I seemed to have difficulty breathing. Then it passed and I warmed up. When I visited the trepangs, they told me that something had gone wrong on the ship. I wondered if Bal had anything to do with it. No, they said, but we must hurry. I had always believed that this ship would last forever. Like the Sun. Dola said they knew a great deal now about the ship's design. And how the Machine worked. They told me they had far more complicated machines at home. But it was difficult to fight the Machine because, as they had done to me, the gloopies had taken the trepangs by surprise.

And without me, they couldn't manage. Was I prepared to assist them further? "Of course," I replied.

Dola explained to me that I would be taking a big risk. If the trepangs succeeded in changing the ship's course or in finding some way to escape from it, they could reach their home planet. But they would not be able to help me.

"You mean there are no records on the ship of a route to Earth?" I asked. They said they didn't know where to look for them, and most likely they were concealed in the Machine's memory. Then I explained my philosophy to them. If they took me with them, I would be willing to go anywhere. It would be far better to live and die among the trepangs than in this prison. Should I fail to escape from here, I would at least take some comfort in the thought that I had helped others. Then dying would be easier. The trepangs agreed with me.

The ship grew colder. I felt the pipes in the small chamber. Barely warm. Two gloopies were fussing with them, repairing something.

I must go now, and I have no idea whether I will return to my notes. I would like to write more—not so much for whoever reads these lines as for myself. If I had been told that someone could be imprisoned for several years without ever seeing another human being, I would have said it meant certain death. Or the individual would lose all human qualities as well as his sanity. Yet it turns out that I haven't. I'm worn out, I've aged, but I live. Thinking back through the years here, I recall that I have rarely been unoccupied. As during my life on Earth. My ability to find meaningful work, to find something or someone that makes life worthwhile is probably responsible for my ability to survive. At the beginning I clung to the hope of returning to my little Olenka, to Earth. Then, when this hope had almost died out, it appeared that I might be useful even here.

The last page. It turned up among a sheaf of blank pages that Natasha had prepared and cut, but had never got to use:

Dear Timofey Fyodorovich!

Warmest greetings. I want to tell you how grateful I am for everything you have done for me and my daughter Olenka. How are you? Are you lonesome? Do you think of me sometimes? How is your health? I do miss you. And please don't ever think that your disability changed my feelings toward you. . . .

Two lines, heavily crossed out, followed. And a sketch of a pine tree. Or a spruce. Poorly drawn.

Several days passed. Pavlysh slept and ate beneath his canopy and continued to explore the ship's long corridors. He rarely used the transmitter and maintained silence when Dag began grumbling, because his comrades perceived Natasha as a sensational phenomenon, an amazing paradox. For them she was an extraordinary discovery. There were no words to describe fully the entire range of their emotions, all of which defied identification.

All of Pavlysh's waking hours were spent alongside Natasha; he walked in her footsteps, saw the ship and its corridors, storerooms, nooks, and crannies—precisely as Natasha had seen them. He absorbed the atmosphere of a prison that most likely had not been designed for that role, a role which had introduced into the life of the Kalyazin nurse a terrifying inevitability—an inevitability which she recognized, but in her heart could not accept.

Now, knowing each word in Natasha's notes, having deciphered the sequence of her movements throughout the ship, having understood their significance, and having explored areas to which Natasha not only lacked access but whose existence she never suspected, Pavlysh could try to deduce what had finally taken place.

Fragments of wire, an overturned robot-gloopy, a dark stain on a whitish wall, the utter devastation in the control room, the imprints on the computer—all these pieces fitted together to form a picture of the ship's last days, events in which Natasha played a role.

Natasha had hastened to finish the last page. Now she regretted that she had recorded so little in the past few weeks. She had never liked to write. Even her sisters had upbraided her for being such a poor correspondent. Only now did it occur to her that, should she escape with the trepangs, the ship might well be discovered by intelligent creatures who would pass her notes on to Earth. But they would curse her for not describing in greater detail her own life and the lives of the trepangs and others on the ship with whom she had contact. Some had already perished, others had ended up in the museum, and the rest were doomed. The trepangs, far more knowledgeable than Natasha in technical matters, knew this: they knew that the reason the ship had been wandering in space for so long, unable to return home, was because something vital had broken down. If the condition persisted, the ship would continue to roam the universe, disintegrating slowly like a dying man.

The last days had been frantic ones for Natasha. She had so many things to do and, although she did not always understand their significance, she realized they were important and necessary for a purpose that was clear to the trepangs. It was pointless to question them. In all those years Natasha had learned that she could not fathom the minds of even the ship's least rational inhabitants, to say nothing of the trepangs. With all the hours she had spent nursing the dragon and living side by side with it, Natasha had still learned nothing about it. Or about the sphere-chiks, living in a glass cube. There were some two dozen of them. At the sight of Natasha, they would often change color and roll along the bottom of the cube like large beads, cutting figures and circles, as if trying to communicate with her. Natasha had spoken to the trepangs about the sphere-chiks, but the trepangs either forgot about them at once or did not have the time to look at them. When it became obvious to Natasha that the journey was nearing its end, she wove a sack out of wires so she could take the sphere-chiks with her.

Even now, as she was writing her last lines and packing her

possessions, she had to interrupt her work and run to open three trapdoors which the trepangs had sketched for her on the map. They were too high for the trepangs to reach.

Natasha realized that they planned to escape on the same launch that had been used to kidnap her. But first they had to check out the ship's Brain; otherwise they could not reach the launch and the Machine would not release them from the ship. Natasha's help was needed here, too.

Natasha had spent a second sleepless night. Not only because she was so excited, but because the trepangs, who never slept at all, could not understand why she had to absent herself and lie down. No sooner would she relax than she would experience a jolting sensation in her head: the trepangs were calling her.

As she packed her diary, Natasha wondered if she should leave it behind. Perhaps it would be safer with her? But who knows what might happen on route? Of course, if she survived, she could always tell her story. Better to leave it, or no trace of her life on the ship would remain.

A jolt in her head. She must run. Suddenly it occurred to Natasha that she would not return here. The slow, monotonous tempo of her life had abruptly and drastically accelerated. At any moment it could end.

"We'll try to turn the ship toward our planet," the trepangs told her. "But it's a very risky business. We must get the ship's Brain to obey us. If we can't, we'll try to disable it so that the rescue launch can be used. But we aren't sure if we can pilot and direct it to where we want it to go. Therefore it's possible we all may perish. We thought you should know."

"I know," said Natasha. "I lived through a war."

The trepangs wasted no time. They fashioned sticks into weapons to disable the gloopies. Natasha was given one and instructed to go ahead of the trepangs and open doors. Two followed her. Two others hastened upstairs to a compartment like a captain's bridge that housed some sort of machinery.

"There are three doors," one of the trepangs said. "But possibly there's no air behind the last one. Or maybe it's different than the air in our compartment. Don't enter immediately. Wait until it fills with breathable air. Is that clear?"

Natasha had ventured beyond the first door once; she remembered the wide passage and the reserve gloopies standing along its walls. Like dead creatures. The trepangs told her that the gloopies rested and were recharged here.

"They won't touch you," said Dola.

"Don't be too sure," said Natasha.

"Please don't take any chances. Without you we can never get out of here. Remember that."

"Don't worry, I won't forget."

Natasha ran her palm along the square in the wall; the door opened. A strange odor drifted through the corridor—a sweetish odor and the smell of something burning.

"They must recharge longer now," said Dola, slithering from behind. "You saw that there were fewer of them in our compartments."

"Yes, I noticed," replied Natasha. "Don't forget to take the sphere-chiks."

"Sphere-chiks?"

"I told you about them."

"Watch out!"

A gloopy leaped from a recess in the wall and went over to them, preparing to block their path and, perhaps, to drive them back.

"Hurry!" Dola cried. "Hurry!"

Natasha ran ahead and tried to leap across the gloopy that had thrown itself at her feet.

But the gloopy—how could she have forgotten this?—bounded up and struck her with an electric charge. Fortunately, it was a weak one; most likely the gloopy hadn't had time to get fully charged up.

Falling to her knees, Natasha let go of the stick. She had hurt herself and groaned in pain; her legs were not what they used to be. And to think she had once played volleyball for the "Medics," who placed second in Yaroslavl. But that was a long time ago.

The gloopy stopped Dola, who also held a stick like Natasha's, but a much shorter one.

"What's wrong?" he asked.

"Nothing," replied Natasha, rising and forcing herself to forget the pain. "Let's go on."

Thirty steps separated them from the next door. Another gloopy began to approach them, but it moved slowly.

"The Machine has already received a signal," said Dola. "They're connected to it."

Hobbling, Natasha hastened to the door. But the square was not in its expected position on the wall.

"I don't know how to open it," she said.

No response.

She looked around. Dola was motionless. A second trepang was fighting off three gloopies with its stick.

"Hurry!" said Dola.

"Maybe there's another approach?" asked Natasha, feeling her hands grow icy. "We can't open this door."

"There's no other way in," hissed Dola. The door was tightly sealed.

More gloopies, flaccid, slow, crawled from their recesses and descended on the trepang.

At that instant the door opened so abruptly that Natasha barely managed to jump aside.

From behind the door sprang a gloopy whom Natasha had never seen before. It was almost as tall as she and, unlike the other gloopies, looked more like a sphere than a tortoise. It had three hinged arms and buzzed menacingly as if to frighten off trespassers.

Suddenly flames shot out from somewhere, sweeping through the corridor and skimming Natasha with their searing heat. Screwing up her eyes, she did not see Dola stop the gloopy with a stick, forcing it to freeze on the spot. But it was too late.

The tortoises, huddled at the other end of the corridor had already blackened, as if charred; and the second trepang, who had held off the gloopies but hadn't jumped clear in time when the door opened, was now a pile of ashes on the floor.

Natasha observed all this as if in a dream, as if totally detached from danger or death. She realized that she must get through the second door. If it closed, Bal and this trepang would have died in vain.

The second door led to a large, circular room shaped like the upper half of a sphere. They entered in time. A second large gloopy began rolling toward the door. Dola managed to reach and disable it before it began to act.

Several doors, all identical, confronted Natasha; she turned to Dola for instructions.

Dola had already rushed ahead and, like a frightened caterpillar, he arched his back high and slithered past the doors, pausing for an instant before each one as if sniffing out what might lie behind them.

"Here, this one," he said. "Find a way to get in."

Natasha was beside him now. This door, too, was unbolted. She pushed it with her hand and it collapsed, as though it had been waiting for her touch.

They stood before the Machine. Before the ship's master. Before the Brain that issued orders to descend on alien planets and seize everything in its path. Before the Brain that maintained order on the ship, that fed, punished, and guarded its captives and booty.

The Machine was nothing but a wall covered with numerous apertures and signal lights, gray and pale blue tiles, and buttons. It stunned Natasha. No—disappointed her, because during all her years here she had often tried to picture the ship's master and endowed him with terrifying traits. It had never occurred to her that the Machine did not have a personality.

A small gloopy, sitting high up on the Machine, slid down and rolled toward them. Dola slithered toward the gloopy and stopped it with a stick.

"Now what?" asked Natasha, catching her breath. Her skirt, sewn from an oilcloth material she had found on the ship, was torn at the knees and bloodstained; apparently she had injured herself badly when she had leaped across the gloopy.

Dola did not reply. He was now standing before the Machine, twisting his little wormlike head as he studied it.

As if in response to Dola's gaze, something clicked, and loud, intermittent hissing sounds filled the room. Natasha recoiled, then deduced that it was the voice of another trepang.

"Everything is all right," said Dola. "Set me over there and I'll turn that knob."

Natasha sat him higher up and he manipulated something in the Machine.

"Listen! Can you hear them? Ours! Ours have control of the main console!" exclaimed Dola, back on the floor again and slithering beside the Machine. "If everything is functioning, we can pilot the ship."

Dola listened attentively to the hissing coming from a black circle—evidently some sort of intercom device—and told Natasha what to do whenever he could not reach various controls on the Machine.

Natasha sat down on the floor to rest.

"They're trying to set the ship on manual control," Dola explained to her after a long pause.

Suddenly Dola let out a scream. Natasha had never heard a trepang scream; something must have frightened him badly.

The lights on the Machine's face went out one after the other, blinking more and more faintly as if bidding each other farewell. The hissing coming through the loudspeaker turned into a weak squeal.

"Hurry! Quickly! To the launch!" Dola shouted.

They had overlooked an important element. Although to all outward appearances the Machine had submitted to the will of the rebelling captives, it retained cells within its memory which ordered it to cease functioning should alien forces attempt to control it.

Dola's pushing and urgent gestures forced Natasha to her feet, but she felt a strange sense of calm as she clung with all her being to one saving thought: "It's all over here. Everything's all right. Now we'll head for home."

Even as she ran behind Dola through the corridor, past

charred gloopies, even as they leaped on deck and Dola ordered her to load the launch quickly with provisions, she continued to lull herself into believing that everything would turn out well. After all, hadn't they overpowered the Machine?

Natasha dropped the provisions by the hatch leading to the launch and ran back again for water and additional air tanks. Dola, forgetting the words he had learned and becoming hopelessly confused, tried in vain to tell her that the Machine had stopped producing air and heat, that the ship would die soon and all would be lost unless they loaded the launch quickly and prepared it for flight.

Two other trepangs hurried from the captain's bridge, dragging some equipment, and began to bustle about the launch.

How long the confusion and rushing about lasted, Natasha could not say, but after her tenth or twelfth trip to the greenhouse, she realized that the ship had grown noticeably colder and that breathing was more difficult. She was surprised that Dola's prediction was becoming a reality so quickly. The ship *was* dying slowly.

Natasha was about to return to her cabin for her possessions when Dola told her they must leave in a few minutes. So instead of fetching her belongings, she decided to get one more air tank; everyone would need air and she could manage without her skirt, kerchief, and cups.

As she dragged the tank toward the launch, she spied the sack she had woven from colored wires. "My goodness," she thought, "I almost forgot." She ran to the launch and dropped the air tank by the hatch.

"Hurry, get aboard!" Dola called out from the launch, rolling the heavy tank into it.

"Hold on," said Natasha, "I'll be back in a minute."

"Now!" shouted Dola.

Too late. Natasha was already running through the corridor toward the sack, then to the glass cube where the sphere-chiks were waiting.

At the sight of Natasha, the sphere-chiks scattered from the center of the cube like camomile petals.

44

"Quickly!" she urged them. "Or we'll be left behind. The launch is leaving."

To her surprise, the sphere-chiks obediently rolled into the sack, making it heavy, heavier than the air tanks. She dragged the sack along the corridor; despite the severe cold, she was sweating and gasping for breath.

Had she not been concentrating so hard on reaching the launch, she would have noticed the sudden appearance of a large gloopy. Ordinarily, it guarded another section of the ship, but sensing that a breakdown had occurred in one of the systems (when the ship was dying), it had rolled through the corridors, trying to locate the cause of the problem.

Natasha was only a few steps away from the launch when the gloopy, who had seen the launch and aimed its fiery ray directly at the hatch, caught sight of her. The ray swung toward Natasha; she had only enough time to toss aside the sack of sphere-chiks.

That one second gave Dola enough time to slam the hatch shut. With the next shot, the gloopy merely blackened the side of the launch. Having exhausted its charge, the gloopy froze above the heap of ashes. It had stopped functioning. The sphere-chiks spilled out of the sack and rolled along the floor.

Dola opened the hatch and realized at once what had happened. But it was impossible to delay their departure any longer. Had he been human, he might have gathered up the ashes, Natasha's remains, and buried them in his homeland. But trepangs are ignorant of such customs.

Dola secured the hatch. The launch separated itself from the dying ship and rushed toward the stars, toward their own solar system.

Pavlysh picked up a charred piece of cloth from the floor, all that remained of Natasha. Then he gathered the sphere-chiks into a pile. The story had ended tragically, although the faint hope remained that he was mistaken. Perhaps, somehow, Natasha had managed to escape in the launch.

He rose and crossed over to the cold, empty robot that had done what was demanded of it, that had stood here all these years aiming into emptiness. The robot had performed its duty, guarding the ship from all possible harm.

"You haven't said a word for about two hours," said Dag. "Is anything wrong?"

"I'll tell you later," said Pavlysh. "Later."

They sat next to the window. Sophia Petrovna drank lemonade; Pavlysh, beer. It was good beer, dark beer. Knowing that you could drink it, that you weren't on active duty, and that the next physical was at least three months away, heightened the delicious pleasure derived from committing a minor, pardonable offense.

"Are you allowed to drink beer?" asked Sophia Petrovna.

"Yes," Pavlysh replied curtly.

Convinced that astronauts did not drink beer, Sophia Petrovna shook her head in disbelief. And she was right. She turned away from Pavlysh and scanned the endless field broken by the quaint silhouettes of spaceships outlined against an orange sunset.

"It seems to be taking a rather long time," she said.

Sophia Petrovna impressed Pavlysh as rather dull, too proper. Studying her sharp profile and her smoothly combed, drawn-back gray hair, Pavlysh concluded that she was probably a very competent teacher of Russian, but he doubted that her pupils cared for her.

"You seem to be studying me," said Sophia Petrovna without turning her head.

"Caught me, didn't you? Professional habit?"

'What do you mean?"

"A teacher has to be aware of everything that goes on in her class, even when her back is turned."

Sophia Petrovna smiled faintly. "And I was sure you were looking for a resemblance."

Pavlysh did not reply. What she said was true, but he didn't care to admit it.

"It seems they are rather late," repeated Sophia Petrovna.

Pavlysh glanced at his watch. "No. Remember, I did advise you to wait at home."

"I couldn't. I was too restless. I had the feeling that someone would pop in at any moment and ask, 'Well, why aren't you on your way?' "

Sophia Petrovna's speech was too correct, slightly bookish, as though her sentences were mentally written out and corrected with a red pencil before they were spoken.

"I have been waiting all these years for this day," she continued, raising her glass of lemonade and studying the bubbles clinging to the sides of the glass. "You might think it strange for me to say that, in view of my efforts to suppress any emotional display of my constant impatience. I waited until the contents of the ship's storage blocks would be deciphered. I waited for the day when an expedition would be sent to the planet inhabited by the creatures that my grandmother called trepangs. I waited for its return. And now that day has arrived."

"That sounds strange," said Pavlysh.

"I know how disappointed you were at our first meeting when I didn't react as emotionally as you had expected. But how else should I have reacted? I only knew Grandmother from several snapshots, from Mother's stories, and the four medals Grandmother had earned as a nurse at the front. To me she was merely an abstraction. My mother is dead, and she was the last person to whom the name Natasha Sidorova meant anything more than a snapshot. Almost a hundred years have passed since Grandmother's disappearance—it was not until you left that I began to develop a feeling for her. No, I can't blame the press, with their stories about the first human being in space. The reason lay in Grandmother's diary. I began to measure my own behavior against her patience, her loneliness."

Pavlysh inclined his head understandingly.

"And young man, I'm not the stuffy old lady you take me for."

Sophia Petrovna's voice suddenly had a totally different ring.

"I am an actress. In our theater I play the role of a cross old lady. And my pupils love me."

"I never doubted that," lied Pavlysh.

Raising his eyes, he met Sophia Petrovna's smile. Her drawn cheeks flushed pink. She lifted her glass of lemonade. "Let's drink to good news."

Catching sight of Pavlysh and Sophia Petrovna from a distance, Dag made his way rapidly between the tables.

"They're on the way," he announced. "The controller received confirmation."

Standing by the window, they watched the planetary launch on the horizon descend toward Earth. Then they hurried below because Dag knew Klapach, chief of the expedition, and hoped to speak with him before the journalists crowded him.

Klapach was the first to emerge from the launch. He halted, searching for someone in the welcoming crowd. A snub-nosed little girl, with fair hair like Klapach's, ran up to him, and he swept her up in his arms. But his eyes continued to search the crowd. As he neared the door he saw Dag, Pavlysh, and Sophia Petrovna. He set his little daughter down.

"Hello," he greeted Sophia Petrovna. "I was afraid you wouldn't come."

Sophia Petrovna frowned. Sensing herself the target of photographers and television cameras, she felt uncomfortable.

A microphone swayed before Klapach's face and he waved it aside.

"Did she make it?" asked Sophia Petrovna.

"No," replied Klapach. "She died on the ship. Pavlysh was right."

"And that's all?"

"It didn't take long to find out about her. Here, look at this."

As the rest of the crew stood behind him, Klapach unbuttoned the pocket of his uniform. It was quiet on the plaza in front of the spaceport.

Klapach took out a photograph. Television cameras focused on his hands, and the photograph filled the screens of TV sets everywhere. Viewers saw a city with squat cupolas and long structures that resembled cylinders and chains of balls. In the foreground stood a statue on a low, circular pedestal. A thin, neatly groomed woman, wearing a sackcloth and bearing a startling resemblance to Sophia Petrovna, held a strange creature, like a large trepang, on her knees.

"Papa," said the little girl. "Let me have the picture."

"Here," Klapach handed it to her.

"It's only a fat worm," said the little girl, disappointed.

Sophia Petrovna lowered her head and walked toward the spaceport waiting room with small, firm steps. No one stopped her or called to her. A journalist started to run after her, but Pavlysh caught him by the arm.

Dag took the photograph from the little girl. He looked at it and saw a dead ship vanishing in endless space.

A minute later the plaza in front of the spaceport rang with voices and laughter and the usual joyful confusion that greets arriving ocean liners or astronauts returning to Earth.

I Was the First to Find You

G ERASSI can't sleep mornings. So today at six, while it was still chilly, he turned on the loudspeaker and asked Marta:

"Are you ready?"

His penetrating voice is as inescapable as fate. It's useless to duck under the covers or jam your head into a pillow.

"Marta," continued Gerassi, "I have a feeling we're going to find something very interesting today. What do you think?"

Marta wanted to sleep. She detested Gerassi and let him know it in no uncertain terms. He guffawed, and the loudspeaker amplified the sound. The captain switched on the intercom and bawled him out: "Shut up, Gerassi. I just came off watch."

"Sorry, Captain," said Gerassi, "but we're about ready to leave for the dig. We can accomplish twice as much in the morning as in the afternoon. And we're racing against time now."

The captain didn't reply, so I threw off the covers and sat up. My feet touched the floor. How many mornings had my feet hit that same worn spot on the rug? I had to get up. Gerassi was right; mornings were the best time to work here.

After breakfast we left the *Spartak* through the cargo hatch. The ramp was badly scratched up by the freight carts. Brown sand and withered branches had drifted onto it during the night. We didn't need space suits; until the heat broke up before noon, masks and light air tanks on our backs were sufficient.

The slightly hilly, desolate brown valley edged up to the horizon. Dust hung over it. The dust seeped into everything: the folds of your clothing, your boots, even under your mask. But the dust is a lot better than the mud. If a passing storm cloud dumps a brief shower on the valley, you have to abandon work and crawl through the slime to the ship, where you wait until the ground dries. Even a jeep is helpless after a heavy shower.

One of the jeeps was waiting for us at the ramp. It was only a ten-minute walk to the excavation site, but time was a crucial factor now. We were planning to leave this planet very soon and had barely enough food and other reserves left for the return journey. We had lingered too long, spending six years on this quest alone. The return trip would take almost five.

Zakhir was fiddling around beside the other jeep—the geologists were going out to do some exploring. We said good-bye to Zakhir and hopped into our jeep.

Gerassi stretched his long legs and closed his eyes. I wondered how a guy who loved sleep so much could wake up before everyone else and rouse the rest of us with that miserable voice of his.

"Gerassi," I said, "you have a miserable voice."

"I know," he said, without opening his eyes. "I've had it since I was a kid. But Veronica liked it."

Veronica, his wife, had died last year. She had been culturing a virus we had found on a stray asteroid.

51

The jeep descended into a hollow enclosed by a plastic shield that was supposed to keep the dust out of the excavation. I jumped out after Marta and Dolinsky. The shields were almost useless; dust, now knee-deep, had drifted in during the night. Gerassi had already dragged out the vacuum cleaner and tossed it into the excavation. Like a living creature, it began to crawl along the ground and devour the dust.

To engage in archeological digs here was insane. Within three days a dust storm could completely bury a skyscraper. In the next three days it could suck out a ditch around it a hundred yards deep. The storms also carried in soot and charcoal particles from endless forest fires raging beyond the swamps. So for the time being, we could not date a single stone or determine when or by whom the settlement had been built. What happened to the planet's inhabitants was a mystery, but we were determined to solve it. So we waited for the vacuum cleaner to finish cleaning up. Then, armed with scrapers and brushes, we would scour the dig for fragments of a vase, a cogwheel, or other evidence of intelligent life.

"They certainly knew how to build," said Gerassi. "It's obvious these storms were a problem then, too."

Yesterday at the dig we had discovered the foundation of a building, or buildings, which had been cut into a rock bed.

"They abandoned this place a very long time ago," said Marta. "If we turn the desert inside out we're sure to find other structures or evidence of them."

"We should have checked the mountains on the other side of the swamp," I said. "We certainly won't find anything here. Believe me."

"But what about the mast?" said Gerassi.

"And the pyramid?" said Marta.

We had spotted the mast on our first flight over the area, but before we landed it had been obliterated by a storm and buried in the bowels of the desert. We had managed to unearth the small pyramid. If it had not been for the pyramid we wouldn't have spent the past three weeks struggling in this dig. It stood before us, flowing into the rock, looking almost as though it had been squeezed out of it. We would take the pyramid with us. Our other finds were a stone fragment and some notches in a rock. No inscriptions or metals.

"They couldn't have lived in those mountains beyond the swamp. Even in the best of times there wasn't any water. And I'd say that this was one of the few places that had some."

Gerassi was right again. The bottomless swamps were impassable, and the mountains inaccessible, as though by design. And then there was the ocean, an endless ocean, storm-swept and nourishing only the most elementary forms of life. Whatever life had once existed here had disappeared, perished perhaps, and now was evolving once again from the most primitive organisms.

We descended into the excavation.

Dolinsky worked beside me. "It's time we headed home," he said, cleaning out a square pocket in the rock. "Do you want to?"

"Of course I do," I replied.

"I suppose I'm not sure how I feel about it. Who needs us there? Who's waiting for us after all these years?"

"When you signed up you knew what you were getting into."

Something glittered in the rock face.

"I knew then and I know now. Sure, when we left we were real heroes. What can be more pathetic than a forgotten hero wandering through the streets, vainly hoping that someone will remember him?"

"It's a lot easier for me," I said. "I never was a hero."

"We can't imagine how the world must have changed in the two hundred years we've been away. That is, if it's still there."

"Hey, take a look at this. I think it's metal," I said.

I was sick and tired of listening to Dolinsky complaining. He was played out. So were the rest of us. All these years we had been sustained by our goals: the exploration of the planetary system and the observation of celestial currents. We lived in hope of making some great discovery. All our efforts had been converted into millions of symbols and dry figures that lay

HALF A LIFE

concealed in the depths of the ship's Brain, in its holds, on its laboratory tables. We had spent our final year rushing about the system, landing on asteroids and dead planets, decelerating, accelerating, realizing that the time for our return trip to Earth was approaching, that the holiday would soon be over. But this one had proved far less festive than anticipated; we had fulfilled our mission, but, unfortunately, we had accomplished nothing beyond it. Though the ship's Brain was jammed with information, the hopes we had cherished during the long years of our voyage had not been realized.

With only a month left, we tackled the last planet. We had to depart for Earth within a month; otherwise we'd never make it. When we had lifted off from Earth, there had been eighteen of us. Now we were twelve. Only on this, the last planet, barely capable of sustaining human life (the others were totally unfit for human habitation), had we found evidence of intelligent life. During the lulls between dust storms, we bit into the rocks, burrowed into the sand and dust; we wanted to learn all we could. Two days remained before we had to depart. Ahead of us lay a journey of almost five years, five years back to Earth—

In the palm of my hand rested a heavy ball the size of a hazelnut. It hadn't oxidized.

"Gerassi!" I shouted. "A ball!"

"What?" A rising wind carried his words away. "What ball?"

A cloud of dust swirled down on us from above.

"Should we wait it out?" asked Marta, picking up the ball. "Hmmm, it's heavy."

"Get back to the jeep," the captain radioed us. "Bad storm coming up."

"Maybe we can wait here until it blows over," said Dolinsky. "We just found a ball. A metal one."

"No, get back to the jeep at once. It's a bad storm."

"If we're really in for a big one, we'd better get the pyramid out of here or it will be impossible to dig it out tomorrow. Then we'll have to leave this place empty-handed."

"We're not going to dig it up. We're leaving it here," said

54

the captain. "We measured and photographed it— Get out of there on the double or you'll be buried alive."

Dolinsky laughed. "Don't worry, we won't be blown away. We'll hold onto our treasures."

Another cloud of dust rained down on us. It settled slowly, circling us like a swarm of mosquitoes.

Gerassi said, "Should we get to work on the pyramid?"

Marta, Dolinsky, and I agreed that we should.

"Dolinsky," said Gerassi, "pull the jeep up over here. It's all set." The jeep was equipped with a hoist.

"I am ordering you to return to the ship at once!" said the captain.

"Where are the geologists?" asked Gerassi.

"On their way back."

"But we can't leave the pyramid here."

"You can go back for it tomorrow."

"These storms usually last two or three days."

Gerassi fastened the hoist cable to the pyramid. I began to sheer off the pyramid's base, using a ray from a cutting torch. The torch buzzed; the stone glowed red and crackled, fighting and resisting the ray.

Directly above us hovered the blackest cloud I had ever seen. The air grew dark; clouds of dust swirled around, and the wind pushed hard, trying to suck us up and whirl us around in the sandstorm. Marta started to help me, but I pushed her away and shouted to her to hide inside the jeep. I tried to follow her from the corner of my eye to see if she had obeyed me. The wind, blowing from my rear, nearly toppled me; the torch jerked in my hand and etched a scarlet scratch along the side of the pyramid.

"Hold on!" shouted Gerassi. "Only a little more to go!"

The pyramid would not surrender. I wondered if Marta had reached the jeep in time. The wind speed above the excavation was incredible. The cable stretched. The captain roared angrily over the transmitter.

"Maybe we ought to leave it?" I suggested.

Gerassi stood beside me, his back pressed against the wall

55

of the excavation. He looked desperate. "Give me the torch!"
he shouted.

"I'll do it myself!"

Like a felled tree breaking off at the stump, the pyramid
suddenly snapped loose and rose into the air like a pendulum.
The pendulum swung to the opposite side of the excavation,
scattered the plastic shields and flew toward us, threatening to
flatten us like pancakes. We barely managed to dodge it. As the
pyramid cut into the wall, a cloud of dust swirled up and I lost
sight of Gerassi. My primitive instinct for survival took over; no
matter what the cost, I had to jump out of the trap, escape from
this hole where the pyramid, straining to tear itself from the
cable's embrace, was crushing everything in sight.

The wind seized me and carried me along the sand like a dry
leaf; I tried to grab the sand, but it slid through my fingers. I was
afraid of losing consciousness from the jolts and blows as I was
dragged along the ground.

The wind rose, tearing me from the earth as if it wanted to
fling me into the clouds, but at that instant a rock blocked my
path and I lost consciousness.

I probably came to rather quickly. It was dark and quiet. The
sand, which had buried me, was crushing my chest and press-
ing against my legs. I was frightened; I was buried alive.

"Calm down," I told myself. "Don't panic."

"Spartak," I called aloud. *"Spartak."*

The radio was silent. It was broken.

"Anyway, I'm lucky," I thought to myself.

If my mask had been damaged, I would have suffocated. I
managed to move my fingers. A minute or two passed—an
eternity—and I knew I could move my right hand. After another eternity I felt the edge of the rock.

Realizing I would be able to dig myself out when my initial
panic vanished, my normal reflexes and sensations returned.

First, the pain. I had been thoroughly battered by the storm
as it dragged me along the ground. On top of that I had been
thrown so hard against the rock that my side was extremely

sore, and breathing was painful, too. I had probably broken a rib. Maybe two.

Second, I became acutely aware of my air reserves. I glanced at the aerometer—there was enough left for an hour. This meant that three hours had passed since the beginning of the storm. I cursed myself for not having taken an extra tank from the jeep. We had about fifty reserve tanks on the ship; each of which would last six hours. We were supposed to have at least two on us at all times. But it was difficult to work in the excavation with an extra tank on your back, so we had left them in the jeep.

Third, I wondered how far I was from the ship.

Fourth—had the storm subsided?

Fifth—had the others made it to the ship? If they had, had they figured out in which direction I had been blown? Did they know where to look for me?

My hand grabbed at emptiness. I crawled out like a mole from its hole, and the wind (the answer to my fourth question was negative) tried to push me back. I squatted beneath the rock, the only refuge in this hell, to catch my breath. The ship wasn't visible; even if it were standing nearby you can't see more than fifteen feet in this dust. The wind was not as fierce as it had been at the beginning of the storm. Or maybe that was wishful thinking. I waited for the next gust of wind to disperse the dust and settle it. Then I would investigate the situation.

Which way should I look? Which way should I go? Obviously in a direction where the rock would remain behind me. After all, the rock had halted my disorderly flight.

I didn't wait for the wind to settle the dust. I walked toward the storm. My air tank would last another forty-five minutes (plus or minus one minute).

Time passed; only thirty minutes remained. Then I fell; the wind rolled me back and I lost another five minutes. At the point when only fifteen minutes were left, I stopped looking at the gauge.

I received an unexpected respite when the air tank, which,

according to my calculations, should have been empty, still had some reserves. I stumbled through the slowly settling dust and tried to ignore the pain in my side because it was certainly not my main problem at the moment.

I tried to breathe evenly, but my respiration was failing, and I kept imagining that the air tank was empty.

Now it was; the air was gone. But at that moment I sighted the ship far away in the settling dust. I ran toward it. Choking, I tore off the mask, although it was a useless gesture, and my lungs were stung by the bitter dust and ammonia—

The locator had sighted me a few minutes earlier.

I regained consciousness in the ship's bay, a small, white, two-bed hospital where each of us had been confined many times during our voyage. For injuries, colds. Or in quarantine. I realized immediately that the ship was preparing to take off.

"Good work," Dr. Grot said to me. "You handled the situation splendidly."

"Are we lifting off?"

"Yes, and you'll have to lie down in the shock absorber. Your bones can't take the G-forces. You have three broken ribs and a torn pleura."

"How are the others?" I asked. "How's Marta? Gerassi? Dolinsky?"

"Dolinsky managed to get to the jeep—he's fine. And Marta is all right, too. She also reached the jeep in time. Fortunately, she listened to you."

"I guess you're trying to tell me—"

"Yes, Gerassi is dead. He was found after the storm, and only thirty steps from the excavation. He was thrown against the jeep and his mask was smashed. We thought you had died, too."

I didn't ask about anything else. The doctor left to prepare the shock absorber for me. As I lay there, I reviewed step by step all my movements in the excavation. I kept thinking how at this or that particular moment I could have rescued Gerassi. I should have said the hell with the pyramid and insisted on following the captain's orders to return.

On the third day after lift-off the *Spartak* picked up speed and headed for Earth. The G-forces had decreased and, released from the shock absorber, I hobbled to the wardroom. Dolinsky was there.

"I've traded shifts with you," he said. "You'll be on watch. The doctor says it's better for you to stay awake for about a month."

"I know," I said.

"Is it OK with you?"

"Why not? We'll see each other in a year."

"I shouted to you to leave the pyramid and run to the jeep," Dolinsky said.

"We didn't hear you. It wouldn't have mattered if we had. We thought we could finish the job in time."

"I passed on the little ball for analysis."

"What ball?"

"You found it. You gave it to me when I went to the jeep."

"Oh, of course. I forgot about it completely. And where's the pyramid?"

"In the cargo hold. Marta and Rano are working on it."

"So I'm on watch with the captain?"

"With the captain, Marta, and Grot. There's not many of us left now."

"An extra watch."

"Right. An extra year for each of us."

Grot entered. The doctor was holding a sheet of paper.

"The results are ridiculous," he announced. "The ball is very, very young—hello, Dolinsky—I say it's just too young. Only twenty years old."

"Can't be," said Dolinsky. "We spent so many days in that excavation! It's as old as the world."

The captain stood in the doorway of the wardroom and listened to our conversation. "Grot, are you sure you haven't made a mistake?" he asked.

"The Brain and I repeated the analysis four times. At first I couldn't believe it myself."

"Maybe it was Gerassi's? Maybe he dropped it?" asked the captain, turning to me.

"Dolinsky saw— I scraped it out of the rock."

"There's still another possibility."

"It's improbable."

"Why?"

"You couldn't have such ruins in only twenty years."

"On this planet you could. Remember how the storm carried you away. And the poisonous fumes in the atmosphere."

"So you think someone got here before us?"

"Exactly."

The captain was right. When Marta sawed up the pyramid the next day, she found a capsule in it. We all crowded in behind her when she placed it on the table.

Grot said, "Too bad we were late. By twenty years. Imagine how many generations on Earth have dreamt about contact with intelligent life in Outer Space. And we were too late."

"Joking aside, Grot," said the captain, "we have made contact. Here it is, right under your nose. We met them after all."

"A lot depends on what's inside this cylinder."

"Not viruses, I hope," said Dolinsky.

"We'll open it in the chamber. With the manipulators."

"Maybe we ought to wait until we get back to Earth?"

"Wait five long years? Oh, no," said Rano.

We all knew that curiosity would eventually get the better of us, that we'd never be able to hold out until we reached Earth. So we decided to open the capsule right away.

"Then Gerassi didn't die in vain," said Marta softly, for my ears alone.

Taking her by the hand, I nodded. Her fingers were cold.

The manipulator's claws placed half of the cylinder on the table and pulled out a scroll. It unrolled stubbornly. We could read the writing on it through the window.

Galactic ship *Saturn*. Identification number 36/14.
Lift-off from Earth—12 March 2167.
Touch-down on planet—6 May 2167 . . .

A text followed but none of us read it through. We didn't have the heart. Again and again we reread the first few lines: "Lift-off from Earth—12 March 2167." Twenty years ago. "Touch-down on planet—6 May 2167." Also twenty years ago.

Lift-off from Earth . . . Touch-down . . . The very same year.

At that moment each and every one of us were struck with the terrible pain of personal tragedy, the tragedy of a useless mission to which our lives had been dedicated, the tragedy of senseless, uncalled-for sacrifice.

One hundred Earth years ago our ship had rocketed into the dark reaches of space. One hundred years ago we had left Earth knowing full well that we would never again see our loved ones and friends. We went into voluntary exile for a longer period than anyone on Earth had ever endured. We knew that Earth would manage very well without us, but we felt that our sacrifices were necessary. Someone had to venture into the depths of space, to unknown worlds which could be reached only through sacrifice. A cosmic whirlwind had thrown us off course, and year after year we had sped toward our goal. We lost our years and counted off the scores of years that had passed on Earth.

"So they finally learned to leap through space," said the captain.

I noticed that he said "they," not "we," although he had always used "we" in the past when he referred to Earth.

"That's fine," said the captain. "Simply great. So they were here. Before us."

He left the rest unsaid; each of us finished it to ourselves. They had been here before us. And managed splendidly without us. In four and a half years, in one hundred Earth years, we would hover over the spaceport (if we didn't perish on the way), and a startled controller would say to his partner: "Hey, take a look at that monster! Where did that brontosaurus come from? He doesn't even know how to land. He'll wreck all the greenhouses around the Earth and smash the observatory mirror! Tell someone to grab the old nag and drag it as

61

far away from here as possible, to the dump on Pluto—"

We retired to our cabins and no one emerged for supper. The doctor dropped in to see me in the evening. He looked very tired.

"I don't know how we're going to make it home," he said. "The incentive is gone."

"We'll make it," I replied. "It will be rough, but we'll make it."

"Attention, all hands!" the intercom loudspeaker rang out. "Attention, all hands!"

It was the captain speaking. His voice was hoarse and wavering, as though he didn't know quite what to say.

"What could have happened?" The doctor was ready for another disaster.

"Attention! Turn on the long-distance transceiver! There's an announcement on a galactic channel."

The channel had been silent for many years: the distance separating us from inhabited planets was so great, it would have been pointless to attempt to maintain radio contact. I looked at the doctor. He had closed his eyes and thrown back his head as if what was happening now was a beautiful dream from which he was afraid to awaken.

There was a rustle and the hum of invisible strings. A very youthful and excited voice began to shout, bursting through to us across millions of miles: *"Spartak, Spartak,* can you hear me? *Spartak,* I was the first to find you! *Spartak,* start decelerating. You are right on course. *Spartak,* I am the patrol ship *Olympia.* I am the patrol ship *Olympia.* I am patrolling in your sector. We've been looking for you for twenty years! My name is Arthur Sheno. Remember it—Arthur Sheno. I was the first to find you! What fantastic luck. I was the first to find you!"

The voice broke on a high note. Arthur Sheno began coughing, and suddenly I saw him clearly, leaning forward toward the microphone in the cramped cockpit of his patrol ship, not daring to tear his eyes from the white spot on his tracking screen. "Excuse me," continued Sheno. "Can you hear me? You can't imagine how many gifts I have for you. The cargo hold is jammed full. Fresh cucumbers for Dolinsky. Dolinsky, can you hear me? Gerassi, Veronica, the Romans are sending you candied fruit cake. We know how much you like it. . . ."

A long silence followed.

The captain broke it. "Start decelerating!"

Protest

TELEGRAMS are always relegated to the bottom of the Olympic Committee's agenda. Everything else has priority, as petty or irrelevant as the matter may be in respect to Olympic affairs.

I have devoted a lifetime to sports. In my youth I set world records. In fact it was I who broke eight feet four inches in the high jump at the Pestalozzi Olympics. Except for sport historians and old men like myself, no one remembers it. The second half of my life has been devoted to the advancement of sports. Someone has to do it. Someone has to adjudicate conflicts between judges and athletic associations, settle disagreements, and gag on synthetic coffee in some godforsaken spaceport.

When I jumped eight feet four inches, millions applauded my feat, and for a fleeting moment I was the most famous person on Earth. Better than that—the most famous in the solar system.

Actually, in every corner of the universe inhabited by humanoids. But I feel I'm accomplishing far more today for the advancement of sports than ever before. My intervention and arbitration have saved many a competition from failure and prevented many decent people from becoming deadly enemies. But for this I hear no applause. I'm just an elderly errand boy, a sports official, and, of course, a grumbler. I am constantly besieged by telegrams which divert me from my appointed rounds, evict me from my bed, and deprive me of the pleasures of a cup of real, nonsynthetic coffee. Rarely do I have a moment's respite to ponder my situation and consider the option of sending the whole stupid shooting match to hell.

While waiting to change ships at the spaceport, I received a telegram. A local official in a too-tight, ridiculous, gaudy uniform approached me and inquired in broken Cosmoling if I weren't the esteemed Kim Perov. I had no choice but to confess that I was.

PLEASE, began the telegram. The "please" is always a tip-off that you're about to be asked to do something your colleagues refuse to do. PLEASE DROP IN [such an apt verb!] ON INIGA. INVESTIGATE ASSOCIATION—45 PROTEST. WELCOME ARRANGED. DETAILS ON ARRIVAL. Signed, SPLESH.

Damn it, why couldn't they have spared a few extra words to tell me who was mad at whom or what parties had to be reconciled? Or at least the location of this Iniga?

I went to the control tower in a rotten mood. There I learned that Iniga was at the other end of the galactic sector and it would have been simpler to send someone directly from Earth instead of fishing me out from the depths of the Galaxy. Secondly, I was informed that there were no direct flights from this point. I would have to fly to a stellar system with an unpronounceable name and change there to a local flight, which most likely had been canceled two years ago.

Having absorbed all these miserable facts, I mentally cursed Splesh and the lot of them on the Olympic Committee and then boarded the ship. I passed the time composing and tearing up an eloquent assortment of letters of resignation. A hobby of mine. I'm the Galaxy's leading expert on the composition of such letters. When I write them, a delicious confidence in my indispensability fills my being.

It was a good thing, too, that the Inigans had been advised of my arrival. A car with five wheels (which had once symbolized Earth's five continents) was waiting for me by the ramp. An official was the first to greet me. My spiritual brother. Maybe even the same age. I even thought his face looked familiar; seems I ran into him at the Plutonville Congress on Olympic Programming.

The rest of the welcoming committee consisted of two lower-ranking sports figures, two young female gymnasts bearing flowers, a girl with green hair, and a gloomy fellow whom I mistook at first for a boxer, then a chauffeur. He turned out to be an interpreter, which we didn't need, because everyone knew Cosmoling.

"Welcome," the chief official greeted me. "I believe we've met before. Weren't you at Berendown at the track-and-field conference?"

I informed my colleague that I hadn't been there but proceeded to inquire no less politely if he hadn't attended the Plutonville Congress. No, he hadn't. We postponed the topic for a more appropriate occasion and, sagging under the two bouquets, I proceeded to the car which I entered with the entire welcoming committee. We spent the next half hour waiting in it while my documents were processed and my baggage delivered.

I would have preferred to familiarize myself at once with the precise details of the problem that required my presence here, but the Olympic Committee's local representative was too busy with my luggage. So, for the most part, I chatted about the weather encountered en route and inquired about Iniga's weather. The interpreter didn't interfere with our conversation; he maintained a gloomy expression as his lips moved silently, translating my words into English and the Inigan official's language into some other Earth tongue. The gymnasts stared straight at me and whispered desperately. One thought kept running through my mind: suppose they had committed such a serious violation of Olympic regulations that they would stop at nothing to win me over to their side? Damn that skinflint Splesh for eternally skimping in his spacegrams. How could I get the facts without displaying to my hosts my abysmal ignorance of the problem that had brought me here?

"Are you too warm?" asked the pretty girl with green hair. I still didn't know if the color was a genetic trait or simply the latest craze.

"No, of course not," I replied, desperately wiping my forehead with my handkerchief.

"I suppose you're very upset about having to change your plans and come all the way out here because of us. Actually, because of me."

"You?"

"We were notified by Splesh himself," interrupted the official, "that you were changing your itinerary on our account. That was really very kind of you. We'll try to make up for it and show you a good time during your free hours. For tomorrow we're planning an excursion to the waterfall. Then we'll have lunch at the summit of Mount Misery."

The prospect of lunch on Mount Misery didn't exactly thrill me, but the few words dropped by the girl shed a welcome glint of light. It meant she was guilty of something. At least I had a scrap of information. So the girl had competed in some event and pulled something there. Well, if that was all there was to it, it would be a lot easier to settle than arguments over the number of competitors or complaints about team accommodations or the wrong system for calculating points. Moreover, the girl looked like an unpretentious kid who was fully aware that she had done something wrong.

Finally my colleague returned and informed me that my luggage was en route to the hotel. I fumbled wildly in my mind for his name but couldn't remember it. Naturally.

As we drove along the smooth highway, my hosts waved their hands, trying to interest me in the beauty of the surroundings. But if you've been through dozens of the Galaxy's spaceports, what's there to see? However, I displayed an appropriate measure of delight. Thus did we reach the city.

It was a typical city. If you've seen one, you've seen them all. As for architectural variations—well, that's a matter of taste. I don't understand that stuff. Anyway, I was exhausted; all I wanted to do was sleep

But driving through the city took longer than the trip from the spaceport. It was bumper to bumper all the way.

"We'll be there soon," said the girl guiltily, as though she were personally responsible for the jams at intersections. Suddenly the brakes screeched. Instinctively I grabbed the armrests and craned my neck to see what had happened.

A large black bird had soared in front of a car about thirty yards ahead of us. I caught my breath. My escorts all began to talk at once; only the interpreter maintained his grim silence. Feeling that I should participate in the discussion, I remarked, "We have similar problems. Birds sometimes cause accidents. Especially with aircraft."

From the horrified way everyone looked at me, I thought I had made an indecent remark, and I pondered the social taboos one encounters from time to time in alien worlds.

About five minutes later we arrived at the hotel, and my hosts suggested that I rest.

"Oh, uh, would you mind leaving the young lady here for a few minutes?" I asked.

Apparently my hosts appreciated my request and nodded approvingly; then they turned and proceeded to the car. The gymnasts dragged the bouquets from the car and handed them to me again. Thus I stood in the middle of the lobby embracing my colorful flowers.

The girl quailed, blushed, and cracked her knuckles, presenting a picture of extreme guilt.

"I'm only going to keep you a minute," I said. "Just one question."

"Of course," she said submissively.

"Would you mind repeating the name of your esteemed chairman?" I asked.

The girl twittered something incomprehensible, so I asked her to print it on a piece of paper. (I must mention here, not without pride, that after several hours of practice I managed to roll off all of the name's thirty-six letters at the farewell banquet given at the end of my stay, upon which I received an overwhelming ovation.) The girl's name was a tongue-twister, too, so I wondered if I could call her Masha. She agreed, although the sound of it had nothing in common with her graceful name, which consisted of some twelve double consonants.

"So," I began, after Masha had finished printing her name on paper, "how do you feel about what happened?"

That was a question I could ask without giving away my ignorance.

"Oh, goodness," exclaimed Masha, "I'm so ashamed of myself! But it was my nerves. It was my nerves that let me down."

"And you let your team down?"

"If only it was just the team, it wouldn't be so bad! But now probably no one from our planet will be allowed to compete."

I was too exhausted to continue the conversation. "All right, you can go now. I'm going to get some rest."

I went to my room and took a shower. So her nerves had let her down. Nothing surprising about that. Almost all sinning athletes blame their nerves. But such a nice girl—

I called room service for coffee. A dark liquid, tasting like burnt rubber, was delivered. I hadn't expected anything better.

"Pardon me," I said to the waiter, "is there any place nearby where I can get a real cup of coffee?"

"But, sir, we serve only the finest, highest quality coffee."

"I believe you, my friend. But would you mind telling me what it's made of?"

The waiter looked at me with deep sympathy and explained that coffee was made from the roots of a certain grass. The roots were dried and ground until they turned a gorgeous violet.

I thanked the waiter, but the look on my face betrayed me. Shrugging, he said, "There's a peculiar brown bean imported here from Earth. Some people actually call it coffee. It's served at the Café Africa, two blocks from here. What crazy fads people will go in for!"

The waiter felt sorry for the snobs who swallowed such weird concoctions. However, my spirits soared, and within five minutes I was on my way to the Café Africa. I had to cross a small park to get there from my hotel, and I took my sweet time, pausing by the shore of a pond rimmed with concrete. The heat had let up somewhat toward evening, making it possible to breathe, and the water had a cooling effect.

On the other side of the pond, a happy mama and papa fussed over their baby in a stroller. The baby appeared to be about a year old—it couldn't walk yet but stood up rather confidently in its stroller, a tuft of hair sticking up from its crown. It burst into happy laughter, which mama and papa promptly echoed. The child reminded me of Yegorushka's youngest grandson, and for a minute I felt as if I were back home.

Suddenly papa took the baby in his arms, kissed it on the forehead, and tossed it into the water. It landed some distance from shore.

I was about to plunge into the water, but before I had a chance to do so, I saw that the parents continued to laugh happily. Either they were crazy or the baby was in no danger. But casual pedestrians who had paused near the pond were laughing too. So was the baby, who splashed about amusingly and didn't sink.

I supposed that Inigan children were taught to swim before they could walk. On Earth, too, there were eccentrics who believed in such things. When I realized this, I calmed down somewhat. But not for long. A few seconds later, the baby's smile vanished as its tiny arms seemed to tire; squealing softly, the child began to sink to the bottom. Only circles appeared on the water's surface—

I did what any decent person would have done. I leaped from the concrete rim and dove into the water. The pond turned out to be larger than it seemed, and the frightened parents were certainly slow to react.

The water was greenish, but rather clean. Seaweed bobbed in my wake, and fish, like dark shadows, swam alongside me through the water. Although the pond didn't seem too deep— about six or seven feet—there wasn't a sign of the baby. I surfaced for air for an instant and caught a glimpse of the frightened faces of the crowd that had gathered around the pond. My wet clothes pulled me toward the bottom. I realized that I was completely out of condition; if I didn't head for shore at once, I'd be the one they'd have to rescue.

When I came up again I saw a smiling papa pluck his smiling cub from the water. With my last breath I made it to shore. I stayed close to the bushes and a good distance from the happy parents. Masha was sitting there on a bench.

"What happened to you?" she asked softly. "Or is that how you Earthlings go for a swim?"

The tone of her voice reflected a pathetic attempt to show respect for the strange customs of my world, where old men normally swam fully clothed.

"Yes," I said through my teeth. "That's the way we do it."

"You do! Aren't you cold now?"

"Of course not," I tried to smile. "I'm warm as toast."

"Where are you going?" asked Masha, trying not to look at me—a drenched old man draped in seaweed.

"For a cup of coffee. At the Café Africa."

"But maybe you ought to—"

"Dry off first?"

"Well, I suppose, if that's customary for you."

"No, it isn't. We normally stroll around in wet clothing," I replied. "But let's return to the hotel anyway, and we'll try to sneak in through the back door since this custom of ours is so shocking to you people."

"It certainly is not!" exclaimed Masha insincerely. But she led me to the back door anyway. Trying to ignore the stares of the curious, I followed the girl obediently.

By the time I got back to my room in the hotel I had dried out somewhat. As I pondered the dissimilarity of our customs, I changed into a dress suit with a large Olympic emblem embroidered on one pocket. I hadn't figured on walking around in evening clothes, but my baggage was quite limited. Well, all right; at least the kid didn't drown.

Masha was waiting for me in the lobby, sitting with her hands folded on her knees, like a mischievous school girl about to explain her behavior to her teacher.

"Are Inigan children taught to swim at a very early age?" I asked, sitting down beside her.

"Swim? Yes, of course."

"Hmmm, that's strange. I've never seen Inigan swimmers compete in our games."

"We didn't join the Olympic movement until fairly recently."

"But you participated in the games, didn't you?"

Masha reddened. The blush, combined with her green hair, produced a curious effect.

"But I was in track and field," she said. "We vouched for anyone in track and field. But it's difficult to do the same for our swimmers. Do you understand me?"

I didn't, but pretended I did.

"Please try to understand me!" Her voice began to tremble. "It was the first time I had ever been in such important tryouts. I give you my word, it will never happen again."

I nodded again, hoping she would let the cat out of the bag.

"Now, because of what I did, Inigans can't participate in the Galaxy Games. Believe me, I alone am guilty. It's all my fault. Punish me. Suspend me. But don't punish an entire planet. Everything depends on you now."

"You know," I said pensively, "I'd like to hear the whole thing from the beginning. It's one thing to read documents and quite another to hear it personally from the parties involved. But don't keep anything back."

Masha took a deep breath.

"After I became Inigan champion of the two-hundred-meter

72

sprint, they decided to send me to the sector tryouts on Eleid. A boy, a jumper, went with me. He did very well in everything. So, anyway, there I was. I took off at the starting line. But an instant too late. Just a split second. You know how it is, don't you? Have you ever competed in track?"

"I was a high jumper," I said. "I did eight-four."

"Wow!" Masha was genuinely impressed.

"But you know what it's like anyway to get a poor start. You run and curse your luck. Actually, I had won the first two heats. So here I am, running and cursing myself, and I feel awfully ashamed because I know they're counting on me and I'm letting them down. Another girl and I tore ahead of the rest, but she was one or two yards ahead of me. I gained half a yard legitimately, and then lost control of myself. I knew only one thing: I had twenty yards to go. Then seventeen— And suddenly, I fleeked."

Masha's eyes were full of tears.

"What? What did you do?"

"I fl–e–e–ked."

Masha started to howl, and I stroked her little green head, trying to console her. "Never mind, dear girl, never mind."

"What's going to happen now?" mumbled Masha. "I can't even look them in the eye."

"Then what happened?"

"Then? Well, all the judges came running up to me and demanded an explanation. You can understand how tempted I was to tell them they had only imagined it. But I told them the truth. And the other team drew up a protest. So did the association. They were absolutely right."

Masha took out a handkerchief and blew her nose. A sheet of paper, folded in quarters, slipped from her purse onto the table.

"Here it is," said Masha. "Here's that awful protest. They wouldn't even begin to hear what I had to say. They wouldn't listen to my promises, either."

Trying to conceal my delight, I took the protest and unfolded it solemnly, as if I were weighing the seriousness of the charges

73

once again. The protest was a lucky catch. I had gone too far in my pose of omniscence to ask what "fleeked" meant.

"For several yards before the finish line," continued the protest after a detailed, useless account of extraneous facts, "Iniga's representative, realizing that she could not catch up to her competitor by legitimate means, flew through the air by turning into a birdlike creature equipped with wings, the form and color of which were not established. After crossing the finish line, the athlete descended to earth again and ran in her natural form for several additional yards before halting."

A lot of superfluous words followed. I sat there rereading the aforementioned sentences, still as much in the dark as ever.

The sudden appearance of the Olympic Committee's chairman jolted me from my trance.

"Well, did you have a nice chat?" he asked, trying to restrain his delight. "I do hope you understand that what happened to her was a grievous misunderstanding."

"Yes," I said folding the protest and tucking it in my pocket. "Yes, I do."

Suddenly, perhaps because I was overtired or my unexpected bath in the pond had affected my nerves, I lost control of myself. I called Splesh the vilest names and confessed to my colleague that prior to my conversation with Masha I had been totally ignorant of the affair. Consequently half a day had been wasted.

This unexpected outburst had a pacifying effect on my colleague and compelled him to revise his image of me from a stern, terrifying inspector to an ordinary man subject to ordinary human foibles.

"May I, sir, explain everything to you in order," he said. "There are so many planets in the Galaxy, I'm sure it's impossible for you to be familiar with the special characteristics of each of them."

"True enough," I agreed. "On one planet they fleek, on another—"

"You're absolutely correct. Evolution on Iniga occurred under far more complicated circumstances than, say, on Earth.

Predators pursued our distant ancestors in the air, on land, and on the sea. They were quick and ruthless. But nature took pity on our ancestors. In addition to intelligence, it endowed them with a very special trait that is also characteristic of many other peaceful creatures on our planet. The victims, like our ancestors, to save themselves from evil enemies, could change the form of their bodies, depending on the environment they were in at a particular moment. Imagine, for example, that a svams is pursuing you. It's a ghastly creature—good thing they're extinct now. So, a svams is about to overtake you in a field. At the instant that you're subject to the greatest nervous and physical stress, your body structure changes and you soar into the air as a bird."

"I understand," I said, although I wasn't sure I did.

"Remember when we stopped short at the intersection and you remarked that birds on your planet could interfere with transportation? Well, we didn't know whether you were joking or not. You know, that wasn't a bird at all. It was only some schoolboy who was about to be run over by a car. At the last moment he succeeded in dodging it by taking to the air."

"Yes," I said, recalling the incident.

"So I'll continue the story. Our ancestors soared into the air to save themselves from the svams. But what awaited them there?"

"Hanggulls," Masha prompted him.

"Correct. Hanggulls," said my colleague. "They would spread their huge black webbed wings and open their black beaks to devour us. What could our ancestors do? They took the only way out: they dived into the water and turned into fish. The body's biological structure underwent change again, in response to an order from an exceptionally highly developed nervous system."

"It's all very clear." I tried not to smile. "Are you born with these traits?"

"Well, now, how can I put it? With the development of civilization, these traits began to die out. But we develop them artificially in our children because they are very useful. You

75

might observe scenes in our city which are incomprehensible to a visitor. Even frightening. If a youngster's potential is not strengthened in early childhood, he will be a retarded freak for the rest of his life."

"Did you say 'freak'?"

"Yes, a freak who is incapable of turning into a bird or fish when necessary. Please rest assured, my dear colleague, that this term does not refer to our guests. We realize that evolution on your planet has taken other paths."

"Too bad," I exclaimed in all sincerity.

I remembered vividly the scene at the pond, so common in their world and so embarrassing for me. My behavior must have appeared ridiculous to the spectators. No wonder the baby's parents hastened to pluck their child from the water; the stupid old geezer might have hurt him by grabbing his fins or gills.

"But"—a tragic note crept into my colleague's voice—"an athlete who wishes to participate in the Galaxy's regular sports events must take an oath. He must swear that he will forget about his unique super-traits. Moreover, we had hoped that no one on the Olympic Committee would learn of—enough of this talk, it's no use—"

"You're right," I agreed.

"Now, after this brief introduction, I would like to invite you to attend track and field events arranged especially for your visit. You will be convinced that we can achieve splendid results without resorting to fleeking."

I rose and followed my hospitable hosts outside.

A bus stopped at the hotel entrance. After all the passengers had boarded it and the doors started to close, I heard tramping noises behind my back. An elderly gentleman with two suitcases was racing through the lobby, clenching a blue ticket in his teeth. I quickly stepped aside. Seeing that the bus was pulling out, the man leaped, turned into a gray bird, and seized the suitcases with his claws. Still clenching the ticket in his beak, he caught up with the bus in a flash, and wedging his suitcases through the door, squeezed inside.

"Well, you see," said my colleague somewhat reproachfully, "sometimes it helps; but—not everywhere."

My eyes were still riveted on the departing bus. "Didn't your ancestors attempt to hide underground?"

"That's pure and simple atavism!" Masha was outraged. "It's too dirty there."

"Oh, but you've forgotten," my colleague corrected her. "What about our geologists?" He turned to me. "Well, what would you say about our future in the Olympic movement?"

"I really can't say yet," I replied.

I pictured the endless meetings of the Olympic Committee as I tried to persuade them to reinstate Iniga, solemnly swearing on behalf of the Inigans that their athletes, in the interest of good, clean competition, would never fleek again. It would be more of a challenge than clearing eight-four, but at least I could do it over a cup of real coffee.

May I Please Speak to Nina?

"**H**ELLO, may I please speak to Nina?"

"This is Nina."

"Nina? Your voice sounds strange."

"Strange?"

"It doesn't sound like you. Are you upset about something?"

"Maybe."

"I guess I shouldn't have called."

"Say, who is this?"

"Since when don't you recognize me?"

"Recognize who?" Her voice sounded about twenty years younger than Nina's.

"Well, OK," I said. "Listen here, I'm sort of calling you about a certain matter."

"You probably dialed the wrong number," said Nina. "I don't know you."

78

"It's me, Vadim. Your Vadi. Vadim Nikolaevich! What's the matter with you?"

"Oh, dear!" sighed Nina, as if she didn't want to hang up. "I don't know any Vadi or Vadim Nikolaevich."

"Excuse me," I said and hung up.

I waited a while before I dialed again. Of course I had reached the wrong party. My fingers hadn't wanted to call Nina, so they had dialed the wrong number.

I dug through the desk for a pack of Cuban cigarettes. Strong stuff, like cigars. They're probably made from cigar scraps.

Why should I have bothered calling Nina? What was there to discuss? Nothing whatsoever. I simply wanted to know if she was home. Even if she wasn't, it wouldn't have changed anything. She could have gone to her mother's. Or the theater; she hasn't been there for ages.

I phoned Nina.

"Nina?"

"No, Vadim Nikolaevich," she replied. "Wrong number again. What number did you want?"

"One four nine—four O—eight nine."

"Mine is G–one—three two—five three."

"I'm way off. Sorry, Nina."

"That's all right. I'm not busy anyway."

"I'll try not to let it happen again. The lines are crossed somewhere, so I keep getting you. The phone system is in very bad shape."

"It certainly is," agreed Nina.

I hung up.

I decided to dial 100 for the correct time—maybe that would straighten out the mess, close some circuit. Then I'd get my call through. "Ten o'clock," announced the time operator. It suddenly occurred to me that if the operator's voice were recorded a long time ago, say, ten years back, she could dial 100 whenever she's home alone and bored; and she'd hear her own voice, the voice of her youth. Maybe she's dead. Then her son or someone dear to her could dial 100 and hear her voice.

I phoned Nina.

"Hello." Nina's voice sounded awfully young. "Is that you again, Vadim Nikolaevich?"

"Yes," I replied. "Our lines seem to be permanently crossed. Please don't get angry. Don't think I'm playing jokes. I dialed very carefully."

"Of course, of course," replied Nina quickly. "I didn't think that for a minute. Are you in a big hurry, Vadim Nikolaevich?"

"No."

"Is your call to Nina important?"

"No, I only wanted to know if she was home."

"You miss her?"

"Well—"

"I understand. You're jealous."

"You're a funny girl," I said. "How old are you, Nina?"

"Thirteen. And you?"

"Past forty. There's a brick wall between us."

"And each brick is a month. Right?"

"Even a day can be a brick."

"True," sighed Nina. "Then it's an awfully thick wall. What are you thinking about now?"

"It's hard to say. At the moment, nothing. I'm just talking to you."

"If you were thirteen, or even fifteen, we could get to know each other," she said. "It would be very funny. I'd say, 'Meet me tomorrow evening at the Pushkin Monument. I'll be there at seven sharp.' We wouldn't recognize each other. By the way, where do you usually meet Nina?"

"It depends."

"At the Pushkin Monument?"

"Not exactly. Sometimes at the Russia."

"Where?"

"At the movie theater, the Russia."

"I don't know that one."

"Sure you do. On Pushkin Square."

"I still don't know what you're talking about. You must be joking. I know Pushkin Square very well."

"It doesn't matter," I said.

"Why?"

"That was a long time ago."

"When?"

She didn't want to hang up. For some reason she seemed intent on continuing the conversation.

"Are you home alone?" I asked.

"Yes. Mama is on the night shift. She's a nurse at the military hospital. She'll be on duty all night. She could have come home today but she left her pass at home."

"All right, then, go to sleep. Tomorrow is a school day."

"You're talking to me as if I were a child."

"Come now, I'm talking to you as I would to any adult."

"Thanks. Why don't you try going to sleep at seven o'clock? Good night, mister. And stop calling your Nina, or you'll get me again. And you'll wake up this poor little child."

I hung up. Then I turned on the TV set and learned that Lunakhod had explored three hundred and thirty-seven meters on the moon in the past twenty-four hours. The research vehicle was busily at work, and I was loafing. After piddling around for a solid hour, I decided to make one last attempt to reach Nina. If I got that girl again, I would hang up immediately.

"I knew you'd call again," said Nina, as she picked up the receiver. "But don't hang up. I'm bored to tears and there's nothing to read. It's too early to go to bed."

"All right," I said. "Let's talk. How come you're up this late?"

"It's only eight o'clock."

"Your watch is slow. It's past eleven."

Nina laughed. A delightful, gentle laugh.

"You're so anxious to get rid of me, it's awful. It's October, that's why it's dark so early."

"Is it your turn to kid now?"

"I'm not kidding. Your watch is lying, and so is your calendar."

"What do you mean?" I asked.

"Now you'll probably tell me it's February."

"Wrong again. It's December," I said. As if doubting my

81

memory, I glanced at the newspaper lying next to me on the sofa. December 23 was the date below the headline.

We were both silent for several moments and I was hoping she would say good-night. But suddenly she asked:

"Have you had supper yet?"

"I don't remember," I said in all honesty.

"Well, I guess you're not hungry."

"No, I'm not."

"But I am."

"You mean you've nothing to eat in the house?"

"Not a thing!" said Nina. "Isn't that ridiculous?"

"I really don't know how I can help you," I said. "Haven't you any money?"

"Very little. And all the stores are closed already. Besides, what could I buy?"

"Yes, everything is closed now. If you'd like, I'll take a look in the refrigerator and see what's there."

"Do you have a refrigerator?"

"An old one," I said. "A Northerner. Do you know that make?"

"No, I don't. Suppose you do find something—then what?"

"Well, I'll grab a cab and bring it to your place. You can meet me downstairs at the entrance."

"Do you live far from here? I'm on Sivtsev Vrazhek Lane, number fifteen, twenty-five."

"I'm on Mosfilmovskaia. Near Lenin Hills. Behind the university."

"I don't know where that is either. It doesn't matter. That was a nice thought and I appreciate it. What do you have in your refrigerator? I'm just asking for the fun of it. Don't take me seriously."

"Hmmm, as I recall— Hold on, I'll take the phone to the kitchen and have a look."

I went to the kitchen with the cord snaking after me.

"OK," I said, "we'll open the fridge."

"You mean you can actually take the phone with you? I never heard of that."

"Of course I can. Where's your phone?"

"In the hall, on the wall. What's in your refrigerator?"

"Hmmm, what's in this package? Eggs. Not very exciting."

"Eggs?"

"Uh huh. Ordinary chicken eggs. Would you like me to bring a chicken? Sorry, it's French, frozen. You'd starve to death before it's done. And your mother will be coming from work soon. Sausage is a better idea. Ah, here's something. I found some Moroccan sardines—a sixty-kopek can. And half a jar of mayonnaise to go with it. Can you hear me?"

"Yes," said Nina very softly. "Why are you teasing me so? At first I wanted to laugh, and now I feel very sad."

"How's that? Are you really that hungry?"

"No, but you know very well how it is."

"What am I supposed to know?"

"You know," said Nina. She paused and then added, "Oh, forget it! Say, do you have red caviar?"

"No, but I have halibut filet."

"Stop! That's enough," said Nina firmly. "Let's talk about something else. I do understand."

"What do you understand?"

"That you're hungry, too. What can you see from your window?"

"From my window? Buildings, a factory. It's eleven-thirty and the shift is ending, and a lot of women are coming out. I can also see Mosfilm. And the fire station. And the railroad tracks. In fact a train is coming along them now."

"You mean you can see all that?"

"Well, the train is quite far away, but I can make out a row of lights—the windows."

"Now you're lying!"

"That's no way to talk to your elders," I said. "I can make a mistake, but I don't lie. So what was my mistake?"

"You said you saw a train. That's impossible."

"What are you saying? It's not invisible, is it?"

"No, it's not, but its windows can't be lit up. In fact, you didn't even look out your window."

83

"What do you mean? I'm standing directly in front of it."

"Is your kitchen light on?"

"Certainly. How else could I dig around in the fridge? The fridge light is burned out."

"Aha! That's the third time I've caught you."

"Nina, tell me what you've caught me at?"

"If you're looking out the window, you've opened the blackout curtains. If you opened the blackout curtains, you turned out the light. Right?"

"Wrong. Why would I need blackout curtains? Is there a war on?"

"Oh, my goodness! How can you lie like that? So you think this is peacetime, do you?"

"Well, I realize there's a war on in Vietnam and the Near East— But I'm not concerned about them."

"Nor am I. Wait, are you a disabled vet?"

"Fortunately I'm all in one piece."

"Are you exempt?"

"Exempt?"

"Then why aren't you at the front?"

Now, for the first time, I began to suspect something peculiar. She seemed to be pulling my leg. Yet she sounded so straightforward and serious about it that she almost frightened me.

"Nina, what front should I be on?"

"What front? Where everybody is. Where Papa is. Fighting the Germans. I'm dead serious, I'm not joking. You have a strange way of carrying on a conversation. Maybe you aren't lying about the chicken and eggs."

"I'm not," I said. "There isn't any front. Maybe I should really come over to see you?"

"And I am really not joking!" Nina almost shouted. "You stop it! At first it was interesting and lots of fun for me, but now I don't feel right about it. You sound as if you're not pretending, but telling the truth."

"Word of honor, I am telling the truth."

"I'm scared now. Our stove is almost out. There's hardly any wood left. And it's dark. All we have is an oil lamp. No electricity today. And I don't like being here alone. I've bundled myself up in all my warm things."

Then she repeated in a sharp and somewhat angry tone: "Why aren't you at the front?"

"At what front?" She was carrying this joke too far. "How can there be a front in 1972?"

"Are you pulling my leg?"

Her voice changed again. Now it was doubting, and, oh, so pathetically small. A forgotten scene rose before my eyes. Something that happened to me long ago, some thirty or more years ago. When I was only twelve. A small stove stands in the room. I am sitting cross-legged on the sofa. A candle is burning, or is it a kerosene lamp? And chicken seems unreal to me. A fantastic bird eaten only in novels.

"Why are you quiet?" asked Nina. "It would be better if you talked."

"Nina, what year is it?"

"1942."

The pieces of the puzzle were beginning to fall into place. She didn't know the movie theater, Russia. And her phone number had only six digits. And the blackout—

"Are you sure?"

"Of course."

She really believed it. Perhaps I was fooled by her voice? Maybe she wasn't thirteen? Maybe this was a forty-year-old woman who had fallen ill in her youth and thought she was still living in 1942, during the war?

"Listen," I said calmly. "Don't hang up. Today is December twenty-third, 1972. The war ended twenty-seven years ago. Do you know that?"

"No," said Nina.

"Sure you do. It's twelve o'clock now— Well, how can I explain it to you?"

"All right," said Nina humbly. "I know, too, that you won't bring me any chicken. I should have known that there weren't any French chickens here."

85

"Why not?"

"Because the Germans are in France."

"There haven't been Germans in France for a long time. Except tourists, of course. But we have German tourists here, too."

"What are you saying! Who let them in?"

"Why shouldn't they be allowed to come here?"

"Don't you dare let such a thought even enter your mind— that the Fritzes will beat us. You're probably a saboteur or spy."

"No, I work for the MAC—the Mutual Aid Council. I deal with the Hungarians."

"There you are, lying again! The Fascists are in Hungary."

"The Hungarians cleared out their own Fascists a long time ago. Hungary is a socialist republic."

"Oh, dear. I was afraid you were a saboteur. Anyway, you're making up these stories. No, don't argue with me. Just go on telling me how things are going to be. Dream up whatever you wish, as long as it's pleasant. Please. And excuse me for being so rude to you. I simply didn't understand."

So I stopped arguing with her. But how could I explain things to her? I pictured myself again, sitting on the sofa that same year, 1942. How I yearned to know when our army would take Berlin and hang Hitler. And, of course, to find out where I had lost my October ration card. So I said to her:

"We'll defeat the Fascists on May ninth, 1945."

"Impossible! That's too long to wait."

"Listen, Nina, and don't interrupt me. I know better than you about this. We'll take Berlin on May second. There will even be a special medal cast—'For the Capture of Berlin.' Hitler will commit suicide by taking poison. Eva Braun will give it to him. Then the S.S. will carry his body to the imperial chancellery courtyard, soak it with benzine, and burn it—"

It was really myself, not Nina, to whom I was telling this. When Nina didn't believe or understand me, I repeated all the facts dutifully; but I almost lost her trust again when I predicted that Stalin would die. But when I told her about Yuri Gagarin, her trust returned. She even laughed when I told her that women would wear bell-bottomed trousers and miniskirts. I remembered the date when our army would cross the Prussian border. I lost all sense of reality. Two children, Nina and Vadim, were sitting before me on a sofa, listening. They were desperately hungry. Vadim was worse off than Nina because he had lost his ration card, and he and his mother had to exist on a single card, a worker's ration card, until the end of the month. Vadim had dropped the card somewhere in the court-yard, and it was not until fifteen years later that he would remember how it happened and would become upset again because the card could have been found. It had, of course, fallen into the basement when he had flung his coat against the grating as he was about to chase a soccer ball.

Later, when Nina tired of listening to what she thought was a fine tale, I said, "Do you know Petrovka Street?"

"Sure. Will it be renamed?"

"No. So listen."

I told her how to go through the archway to the courtyard and where she would find the basement covered by a grating. And if, as she insisted, it was mid-October 1942, most likely my ration card would be lying in the basement.

"How awful!" said Nina. "I couldn't stand it if I did. You must look for it right away. You must."

She, too, entered into the spirit of the game, and somewhere reality vanished; neither she nor I could understand in what year we were living. We were outside time, but closer to her 1942.

"I can't find the card," I said. "It was too many years ago. If you can, go there. The basement should be open. If neces-sary, say it was you that lost the card."

At that instant we were disconnected.

Nina was gone. I heard static. Then a woman's voice said:

"Is this one four three—one eight—one five? We have a call for you from Ordzhonikidze."

"Wrong number," I said.

"Sorry." The woman's voice was indifferent.

Then came a series of short buzzes.

I dialed Nina's number again. I had to apologize to her, and laugh with her again, though it was all quite silly.

"Hello," said Nina's voice. The other Nina's.

"Nina?" I asked.

"Is that you, Vadim? Why aren't you asleep?"

"Sorry," I said. "I'm trying to reach another Nina."

"What?"

I hung up and dialed again.

"Are you out of your mind?" asked Nina. "Have you been drinking?"

"Sorry," I said and hung up again.

It was useless to try again now. The call from Ordzhonikidze had cleared the lines and everything was normal again. I wondered what little Nina's real number could be? Arbat 3; no, Arbat 1–32–30 . . . No, 40—

Big Nina phoned me herself.

"I stayed home all evening," she said. "I thought you'd call and explain why you behaved so strangely yesterday. Obviously you're clear out of your mind."

"Probably," I agreed. I didn't want to tell her about my long conversations with the other Nina.

"What's going on? Who's this other Nina?" she asked. "A character in a novel? Are you trying to let me know you want me to be something else?"

"Good-night, Ninochka," I said. "I'll explain everything to-morrow."

The most interesting aspect of this strange episode is that its ending was no less strange. The following day I visited my mother. I told her I would clean up the attic. I had been promising to do it for three years, and here I was at last. I know that Mama never discards anything—who knows what might come in handy some day? For about an hour and a half I dug through old magazines, textbooks, and the like. Finally I came across a 1950 telephone book. It bulged with notes and paper markers; its edges were frayed and soiled. I knew the book so well that I wondered how I could have forgotten about it. If it were not for my conversations with Nina, I would never have remembered it. I felt slightly ashamed, as one does about a worn-out suit which is sent to certain death when donated to a junk dealer.

I knew the first four figures. G-1-32. I also knew that the telephone, if neither of us had been pretending and she hadn't been pulling my leg, was located at 15–25 Sivtsev Vrazhek Lane. There wasn't the slightest chance I would find that phone. I dragged the stool from the bathroom and sat down in the hall with the phone book. Mama, who hadn't the vaguest notion of what I was doing, only smiled as she passed me and said, "It's always the same with you, Vadi. You start to sort through the books, and ten minutes later you're reading. And that's the end of the cleanup."

She didn't notice that it was the phone book I was reading.

I did find the number. In 1950 it was at the same address as in 1942. It was registered under Frolova, K.G.

True, the whole thing seemed ridiculous. I was looking for something that couldn't possibly exist. But even so, I went to Sivtsev Vrazhek Lane.

The apartment's new tenants did not know where the Frolovas had gone, but at the building manager's office I was lucky. An elderly bookkeeper remembered the Frolovas, and with her assistance I obtained all the necessary information through the address bureau.

It had grown dark. A blizzard swirled amid identical wainscotted towers in the new neighborhood. An ordinary two-story market was selling French chickens in transparent, frost-coated packages. I was tempted to buy one and take it to Nina as I had promised, though it was thirty years too late. It was a good thing I didn't. Because no one was home. From the buzzer's echoing sound, it appeared that the apartment was empty and that the tenants had moved out.

I was about to leave but, since I had come this far, I decided to ring a neighbor's bell.

"Excuse me, please. Does Nina Sergeevna Frolova live in the next apartment?"

A teenager in a T-shirt, holding a smoking soldering iron, replied indifferently: "They went away."

"Where to?"

"North—a month ago. They won't be back till spring. Both of them—Nina Sergeevna and her husband."

I apologized for disturbing him and was about to descend the staircase. I thought to myself that it was entirely possible for more than one Nina Sergeevna Frolova, born in 1930, to be living in Moscow now.

Suddenly the door behind me opened again.

"Just a minute," said the same boy. "My mother wants to tell you something."

His mother appeared in the doorway, drawing her housecoat around her more tightly.

"Who are you to her?"

"Just a friend," I said.

"Not Vadim Nikolaevich?"

"Yes, Vadim Nikolaevich."

"Well, now!" The woman was delighted. "I almost let you go. She never would have forgiven me if I had. Those were Nina's very words: 'I won't forgive you.' She tacked a note on her door, but the kids probably tore it down. She said you'd come in December. And she said she'd try to come back then, but it was so far—"

The woman stood in the doorway, looking at me as if I would now reveal some secret, tell her about an unfortunate love affair. No doubt she had tried to wheedle it out of Nina with "Who is he to you?" and Nina had also replied, "Just a friend."

The woman paused and drew a letter from the pocket of her housecoat.

Dear Vadim Nikolaevich!

I know, of course, that you won't come. How can I believe childhood dreams that even I find completely impossible. Yet your ration card was in the basement—

90

Red Deer, White Deer

*L*UNIN put into shore for the night. It was a good spot—a high bank covered with old trees. Below the bluff stretched a broad sandy beach. The sand was firm along the water's edge; closer to the bluff, where it was warmed by the sun, it was soft and crumbly. Trunks of trees that had fallen down from above were scattered about in the sand. The river was slowly eroding the high bank. Lunin tied the launch to a gnarled black stump whose roots had spread into the water, and the boat bobbed gently on a shallow wave.

He decided to erect his tent on the bluff—from the way the treetops bent in the wind he knew he would not be troubled by mosquitoes up there—and slinging the tent over his back, he began his ascent. The cliff had been formed from porous sandstone and solidly packed but treacherously unstable quartz sand. Lunin grabbed hold of roots and thorny bushes for support, but they broke loose with such surprising ease that he had to hug the cliff to keep himself from sliding back.

Lunin could have stayed below and spent the night on the launch, but he looked forward to a relaxing evening on land, to leisurely contemplation, to mentally sorting out the day's trophies. The trophies were in the launch, but Lunin knew them by heart. More important than the trophies themselves, however, was the confirmation they might provide to ideas still too nebulous to be called theories.

A fresh wind, growing in intensity, blew above the mirrorlike river. The distant shore had already been swallowed by the gloom. The wind drove away the mosquitoes. After he erected the tent and had a snack, Lunin settled back against a gnarled stump and dangled his legs over the edge of the cliff.

Somewhere in the distance birds were calling to each other. A bough snapped. Lunin heard the sounds of the forest but wasn't disturbed by them; he knew that if necessary he could reach the tent with a single leap and turn on the force field. He bent over and looked at the launch. It was safe. From on high the launch seemed so tiny, like a bug washed ashore by a wave. Loneliness, which pursued him like a disease, was about to assault him again. He was a stranger on alien territory, as were the other geologists a thousand miles away, sitting beside their tents and listening to the sounds of the forest or plain; as was the botanist spending the night somewhere alone.

Lunin looked up, seeming to sense the Station flying directly overhead at this very instant. The Station was like a tiny bright star, no more than a speck in the sky. By poking his head inside the tent he could call the Station and ask, for example, about tomorrow's weather. They'd give him a report and bid him good-night. The Station's controller was bored stiff; he couldn't wait for his turn to come down. He was a geologist, or geophysicist, and had the illusion that he would never have time to feel lonely on such a rich and interesting planet. Maybe the controller was right and he, Lunin, was an exception. This planet could have been different. Quite different. Perhaps

Lunin was tormented by loneliness for one reason—he had learned the planet's terrible secret.

Lunin, the Station's only paleontologist, had initially worked with a team of geologists. Then he had left them. He engaged in only the most preliminary explorations and could only guess what to expect. Nothing more. It would be up to others to follow up with systematic investigations and make whatever discoveries there were to be made. Chance and guesswork were Lunin's lot, and one of those chance finds had occurred yesterday. And then a second one this morning—when he had found a second site. It appeared to be no older than yesterday's—

A strange grunting sound came from the underbrush. It could have only one meaning: a signal to attack. Lunin rushed toward his tent, thinking how fortunate it was that ploogs never attacked silently. You always had the luxury of contemplating your situation for all of a second. But not a fraction more.

He couldn't make it to the tent in time. The ploogs rushed at him from behind the trees and also swung down from the treetops. As Lunin stumbled beneath the weight of their hot fur, he reached the knob for the force field and activated it. The field pressed his legs to the ground. He jerked his legs hard, trying to draw them in. It wasn't easy; one of the ploogs had managed to hook his paw into Lunin's boot and pull it toward him. Meanwhile, the others—three or four—pounded against the invisible wall separating them from Lunin.

The disproportionately large eyes of the ploogs, glowing red in the darkness, lent a deceptive quality to their fierce expressions: the eyes didn't seem to go with their bared fangs and the wrinkles puckering the sparse fur on their low, sloping foreheads. Instead, the eyes had a surprised, confused, even doleful expression. But ploogs were utterly devoid of compassion. They were invincible, sullen predators, masters of the night world. The size and shape of their eyes were a necessity, enabling them to see in almost total darkness.

Lunin's boot remained in the ploog's grip, although the prize turned out to be an unappetizing meal. But another, rather larger, ploog became intensely jealous. So the beast forgot about Lunin, who knew, however, that the ploogs would return soon. Meanwhile they were tearing his boot apart.

Lunin planted himself at the entrance to the tent and fumbled behind for his movie camera. The beam of light thrown by the camera picked out only an enormous black mass swerving and swaying like a giant swarm of bees; the ploogs were locked in combat. Suddenly, from behind a tree, a full-grown male ploog emerged. Walking on hind legs with firm confident steps, he ignored the trivial quarrel. Far more attractive to him was the bigger prize—the tent and the man inside.

The ploog ignored the light; his pupils contracted to the size of pinpoints. An involuntary smile flitted across Lunin's face as he drew in his unshod foot and watched the beast through the camera's viewfinder. (Some days ago when the first photographs of these enormous apes had arrived at the Station, Dr. Leontiev from the *Cosmos* had remarked with a very straight face that "Gustav Ploog was there." Everyone knew Gustav Ploog, chief physician on *Earth-14.* He had a remarkably angelic disposition but a most intimidating appearance. He looked like a gorilla. With glasses. So Leontiev had added a pair of specs to the photograph, and the pithecs were dubbed ploogs.)

"Well, hello there, Doctor Ploog," said Lunin, approaching the beast slowly. "So you think I'm a pretty easy catch, eh? Well, buddy, you've got another guess coming."

For an instant Lunin feared that the force field might not be working, so he pulled his bare foot out from under him and thrust it forward. It hit the barrier. It would be tough going barefoot for long here, so tomorrow, thought Lunin, he would fly to the Station.

The chief of the ploog herd had spread his paws on the invisible wall and pressed his nose against it. Frustrated, he moved off in a rage. The sight of a man had triggered memories in the beast, memories that were also responsible for killing Lunin's curiosity about the ploogs. Today Lunin had encountered something which confirmed his well-founded suspicions. The sites.

So far he had stumbled across two of them. The one yesterday was on the slope where several shallow caves looked out on a grassy meadow. Lunin had detected traces of soot in one of the small caves; and beneath bat droppings on the floor lay kitchen middens—broken bones, ashes, and fragments of flint. About an hour and a half later, having recovered his equilibrium and rested after fussing around with his cameras and fixatives, Lunin had called the Station and reported his find. His voice sounded so normal and calm that the controller on duty had not realized the significance of the message.

"I'm recording the coordinates," the controller had replied indifferently, as he did several times a day to various groups calling in. Each of them firmly believed that its find would go down in history. "Paleolithic site . . . preliminary analysis of kitchen middens . . . eighty to ninety years, plus or minus five. . . . Hold on. What kind of kitchen middens?"

"Bones," said Lunin. "Ashes."

"What do you mean?"

"Did you get the message? I'm going back to work." Lunin signed off. He visualized the excitement that would sweep through the Station and tear physicists, astronomers, and zoologists from their work. It would spread below to the planet and be picked up by the teams working there. "Hey, did you hear what Lunin found?"

Nothing happened for the next five minutes, but Lunin wasn't deceived by the silence. He sat on a boulder and awaited the backfire.

"Lunin," came a voice through his receiver, "can you hear me?"

It was Vologdin, chief of the expedition.

"I've got you," said Lunin, chewing on a blade of grass.

"Are you sure you haven't made a mistake?"

Lunin ignored the suggestion.

"Lunin, why don't you answer?"

"You got my message."

"But are you sure?"

"Dead sure."

"Should we send a team down?"

"Not for the time being. Nothing special has happened."

"Great."

Lunin could imagine the Station's entire complement standing behind the chief and listening to the conversation. "Listen, Vologdin," he said. "I found a Paleolithic site all right. But I don't know who inhabited it. It looks recent. So if there is intelligent life on this planet it's still in the caveman stage. Otherwise we would have found it long ago."

"How come no one saw any evidence before?"

"Look, how much do we really know about this planet? We've been working here only two months. And we're just a handful."

"But we've filmed every square inch of the planet, and any evidence—"

"They probably live in the forest."

"Maybe it's the ploogs?"

"Don't count on it. Li will give you all the dope on them. He followed their herds for two weeks. They're monsters, a little better organized than gorillas, but ten times more vicious and stronger. They manage very well without fire."

"Can you handle everything all right?"

"Sure. You can send down a capsule. I'll put the film in it, and you can take a look at it yourself. But I'm not promising you anything sensational."

"We'll send it down right away. I think you're underestimating the significance of your discovery."

"I wouldn't even call it a discovery. I stumbled across the site by chance. Anyway, I'm going down the river now. Maybe I'll see something else."

Exactly twenty minutes later the capsule had arrived for the film. By then Lunin had gone over to the launch for dinner. The capsule contained a note from Li—a personal note. "Finishing up my work on the subject day after tomorrow. Can join you

96

then." Lunin didn't bother replying. If Li could make it, he'd come.

The Station had contacted him about ten times that day. From the excitement, one would have thought he'd uncovered a major city rather than Paleolithic remains.

Thus had the day passed. Then this morning he had discovered the second site. Perhaps he had missed evidence of the Paleolithic stage before because he hadn't counted on finding it. He had been searching for a Cenozoic site, and in one place had stumbled upon a Triassic site. His eyes hadn't looked for traces of man, but then, like radar, they began to scan everything around him. Was that a chip on a piece of flint? That dark spot on the cliff—could that be the entrance to a cave?

The site turned out to be a small one, the refuse scanty. Then, in a hole half filled with sand, Lunin found the first skull. And the remains of a skeleton. The skull had to be pieced together; it had been smashed to bits by a predator's powerful teeth. Or, perhaps, by a kinsman's. The site had definitely belonged to humanoids.

Circling the site, Lunin found several more human bones. He was right—in no way were the site's occupants related to the ploogs. Half the size of ploogs, with much finer bones, sloping foreheads, and receding chins, they were much closer to intelligent creatures than were the apes. He could assume that they had been attacked, and that their enemies had not only killed them, but devoured them as well.

After spending several hours collecting and preserving his trophies with fixatives and conversing with visitors rushing in on launches and landers, Lunin pushed on further. By then he was beginning to have his suspicions about the sites, but couldn't confirm them. Bearlike animals and predators resembling enormous wolves prowled through this area. But, according to Li's findings, neither species seemed to live in groups. It was extremely doubtful that they could have killed all the site's occupants, who numbered more than ten—killed them and literally torn them to shreds. That left only the ploogs.

Now, as he sat in his tent minus one shoe and looked at the raging ploog foaming at the mouth, Lunin was filled with hatred.

Nature is cruel to intelligence. Still untempered and unaware of its potential strength, intelligence finds itself surrounded by powerful enemies; it hovers always on the brink of extinction. Enemies, both here and on Earth, are always more insolent and equipped with sharper and bigger teeth than the forebears of intelligent creatures. One must outwit them, hide from them, survive—on the other hand, without powerful enemies one's intelligence would not be sharpened.

The ploog continued to struggle for its booty. Now Lunin had the feeling that the ploog identified him with the troglodytes and viewed him not only as booty but as his worst enemy, a creature with whom he could not share power on this planet.

Soon the chief ploog was joined by the others, who happily were through with the boot. Finally, when Lunin had had enough of their shaggy, angry faces, he delivered a blinding flash with his blaster. To his satisfaction, they immediately scattered.

Unable to fall asleep quickly, he radioed Li, who had by now completed his investigation of the scratches on the human bones. The marks matched the ploogs' teeth, confirming Lunin's suspicions. When Lunin finally fell asleep, he realized that his situation on this planet had changed. No longer was he only a research scientist; now he must assume the additional role of protector of the weak. Probably very few people were left here. The ploogs had proved to be more dangerous than cave bears had been to our ancestors.

The following day Lunin had to return to the Station because of his boot. He couldn't see himself radioing the controller and asking: "Do me a favor and send out the capsule with a right boot, size ten, preferably black. The ploogs chewed up mine." Besides, he wanted to consult with Li and the chief, and also requisition a lander for several weeks so that he could reconnoiter the river basin at zero altitude.

Three weeks later, Lunin and Li had explored the basin and

returned to the Station to analyze the material. They tried hard to refute the conclusions toward which their latest finds were pushing them.

The ploogs had arrived here fourteen hundred years ago. Quite recently. Perhaps from another continent where there were many of them. By that time the first humanoids on the planet knew how to chip stone and make fire, but they were unprepared for combat with enormous apes organized into raging herds, with beasts who saw equally well by day or night, with enemies whose skin was too thick for their stone-tipped spears to pierce.

One after another the handfuls of people scattered through the forest fell victim to savage attacks. The abandoned, devastated sites were fifteen hundred, a thousand, and eight hundred years old. On the shore of a large shallow lake, among fingerlike projections from the rocks, Lunin found the site of one of the last, if not *the* last, battle, which had taken place five hundred years ago, plus or minus ten years. More than eighty people had perished here. The bones of ploogs were scattered about too. Evidently, people had learned to band together— but too late. Lunin and his colleagues could call a halt to their search. Not a single human being remained on the planet.

"Too bad we didn't get here sooner," said one of the physicists. "We could have covered them with a force field."

"Five hundred years ago?"

"Who knows? Maybe as recently as last year the remaining survivors were hiding here. We really don't know."

"I doubt it," said Li.

"I suppose you're right," said the physicist. "Still, you have to feel sorry for them."

The next day Lunin spotted a large site by the cliff; black concretions had fallen out of the pinkish sandstone onto the shore, and ammonites projected from the cliff like the curled horns of mountain rams. There he found a cave, the scene of a battle that had taken place some eight hundred years ago. Probably it had been a brief one, and like all their battles, at night, when, by the light of a fire, ploogs whirled around and roared near the cave. Breathing heavily and repulsing blows from spears, the ploogs had dragged away the boulder blocking the cave's entrance.

Lunin explored every inch of the cave for traces of habitation. He picked up a fishhook made of sharpened bone and found a hollowed-out stone into which water dripped from the cave's ceiling. A second, remote entrance to the cave was wide enough for the sun to light up the flat sandy floor and smooth walls. A rough-hewn stone lay by one wall. Above it were drawings. The first drawings found on the planet. Lunin held his breath as though afraid the drawings might crumble and vanish if he exhaled.

Someone had chosen this wall to express his wonder to the world, to capture motion and to cast a spell over it with his magical power, a power flowing from the unity of his world and his growing mastery over it. He had drawn a bear, humpbacked, with vertical stripes beneath its belly representing long fur. Near the bear were funny little stick figures, of men, running somewhere. There was also a drawing of a boat, with a sun above it. Sandstone and chalk had suggested the use of color to the artist. The sun was red; the little men, white.

Lunin moved slowly along the wall, reading all the drawings. A black ploog—a small one—round-shouldered, teeth bared. Beside it was a man who had thrust a spear into the beast. The drawing was pure fantasy; their art, still at a primitive stage, had begun to dream.

Lunin wilted. He remembered that he had left the camera in the lander and would have to return for it.

Before returning to the lander he looked outside the cave's entrance for other drawings and found one. A flat overhang above the wall at the entrance had protected the drawing from the rains. This one was larger than the others, the lines freer, as if the artist, once outside the cave, could safely depart from conventions that were developing hand in hand with an emerging art.

It was a deer. A red deer, the instant of its leap captured by the artist's memory and rendered with an airy, casual touch.

Lunin ran to the lander for his camera. Although pained by what he had seen, he was reconciled to the conclusion that nascent intelligent life on this planet had perished. Now that he was confronted by a historical fact, his sorrow and even his hostility toward the ploogs were no longer abstractions.

The existence of the deer, its airy leap, had refocused his thinking. The finality of this tragedy, the end of intelligent life, affected Lunin in an intensely personal way. It generated other fears: now he was afraid the red deer might be destroyed. By an earthquake, or rain, or some other powerful force.

Turning on the transmitter briefly, he delivered a cryptic message: "I found cave drawings. I'll photograph them and spray them with fixative. I'll contact you later. Wait." He grabbed the camera and fixative and hurried back, walking rapidly but cautiously, trying not to trample the bones and stone fragments. A few steps away from the cave's second exit, he stopped short. Someone was there. Now he could clearly hear heavy breathing. He slung the camera over his shoulder and placed his hand on the blaster, which was loaded with paralyzing cartridges. The snorting continued, sounding like a small locomotive raising steam beneath the cliff. Lunin reached the end of the cave on tiptoe and looked out.

His worst fears were realized. An enormous black ploog was squatting in front of the drawing of the red deer, trying to destroy it. Lunin raised his blaster. It wasn't too late, but he held his fire. He had noticed a piece of chalk in the ploog's paw.

Breathing hard, howling and baring his teeth, the ploog scratched the chalk along the wall directly beneath the red deer. His paw shook from the effort. He had produced a nearly straight horizontal line from which short sticklike lines projected upward. There were four sticks of varying lengths, one of which failed to meet the horizontal line; so the ploog began to poke the chalk at the wall, trying to join the stick and the line with white dots before continuing his exhausting labor.

Lunin realized what the ploog was trying to draw on the wall. A deer. The same deer as the original, but white and flipped over on its back. A dead deer, slaughtered for food.

The ploog had undertaken a task beyond his powers; neither his paws nor eyes were ready to reproduce a work of art, particularly an artistically revamped version.

At the end of the horizontal line, the ploog pushed the chalk around, creating a star-shaped object. The deer's head. No matter that it didn't resemble a head: both Lunin and the ploog recognized artistic license.

The ploog moved away from the wall, tilted his head to one side, and stood motionless, admiring his creation. Vanity was beginning to stir in the beast. In the sticks he saw the huge, still-warm carcass of a deer; therefore he was not interested in comparing his creation with that drawn by his vanquished enemies. Now the deer could not escape; it had been toppled.

Lunin's feelings toward the beast began to change; he felt strangely grateful, almost tender. He took a step forward. At that instant the ploog happened to glance around as if seeking an audience for his labor. The man's and beast's eyes met.

The ploog forgot about the deer. Senseless rage and fear flared in the surprised beast's enormous round red eyes. Evolution, which had taken an unexpected step forward, was still too weak to hold its new ground, and the step was forgotten for the time being.

Having nothing better at hand, the ploog flung the chalk at Lunin. It left a white spot on the chest of his space suit, then bounced off and hit the wall. Instinctively Lunin recoiled behind a ledge.

When he looked out again he saw only a black spot, the back of the ploog as it tore its way through the brush.

The black spot disappeared. The leaves trembled as though struck by a gust of wind. The sounds of snapping twigs subsided.

Lunin turned around and faced the cliff. In the shade the stone appeared lilac-colored, and on it glowed the figures of two deer. One red, one white.

Snowmaiden

ON L Y once did I see a ship die.

It is not as terrifying as it sounds, because the reality of it doesn't register quickly enough to shake you up. From the bridge of our launch we watched them trying to land on the planet. For a moment it seemed they would make it. But they were coming in too fast.

The ship touched the bottom of a sloping hollow and continued to move as if determined to penetrate the rock wall. But the rock face refused to submit to metal; the ship began to disintegrate like a drop of water splattering on glass. It slowed down; various parts broke off sluggishly and soundlessly from the ship's body and, scattering over the valley like dark blotches, searched for a convenient place to land and die. Seconds later its seemingly interminable motion had ceased. The ship was dead, and only then did my brain belatedly reconstruct the thunder of splitting bulkheads, the groans of tearing metal, and the screaming air. The living creatures aboard the ship probably never heard more than the very beginning of these sounds.

A ruptured black egg, greatly enlarged, appeared on the screen, and patches of frozen albumen surrounded it like a quaint border.

"It's all over," someone remarked.

We had received the ship's distress signal and almost reached it in time. We saw it perish.

The scale and horror of this spectacle did not strike home until we had lowered the launch and stepped out into the valley, where, at close range, it acquired human proportions. The dark blotches turned into chunks of metal the size of a volleyball court; the engine parts, nozzles, and sections of the braking shafts, into the broken toys of a giant. It looked as though someone had thrust a gigantic paw into the ship and disemboweled it.

About fifty yards from the ship we found a girl. She was wearing a space suit; all aboard, except the captain and the watch officer, had managed to don their gear. Obviously the girl had been close to the hatch, which tore off on impact. She was thrown clear of the ship, like an air bubble fizzing off a goblet of mineral water. The miracle of her survival was another of those flukes that have occurred repeatedly since man took to the air. People have fallen from planes five miles above the earth and managed to land, almost unscathed, on steep, snow-covered slopes or in the tops of pine trees.

When we carried the girl onto the launch, she was in shock, and Dr. Streshny would not let me remove her helmet, although we all realized she might die if she didn't receive medical attention. The doctor was right: we knew nothing about the composition of their atmosphere, nor did we know what sort of viruses, deadly for us but harmless for her, lurked in her fair, shiny bobbed hair.

I should describe the girl and explain why I, and everyone else, considered the doctor's fears not only exaggerated, but of no real significance. We normally associate danger with creatures whose appearance is disturbing to us. As far back as the twentieth century, a psychologist stated that he had developed a reliable test for astronauts venturing to remote planets. The subject had only to be confronted by a repulsive-looking six-yard-long spider. The subject's instinctive reaction would be to draw his blaster and empty a full charge into the spider—but the spider could very well prove to be a local poet wandering about in solitude, discharging his responsibilities as secretary of the Voluntary Society for the Protection of Birds and Butterflies.

To expect anything insidious from this slender girl, whose long eyelashes cast a shadow on her pale, delicate cheeks, whose face stirred in each and every one of us an overwhelming desire to see the color of her eyes—to expect anything insidious from this girl, even in the form of viruses, would have seemed most unchivalrous.

Although no one actually said as much, we all sensed that Dr. Streshny felt like a scoundrel, like a petty bureaucrat intent on carrying out his instructions to the letter, who was denying an invalid permission to receive a visitor.

I wasn't present when the doctor sterilized the probe he would use to pierce the space suit and collect an air sample. Nor did I learn the results of his efforts immediately, because we had left our ship for another trip to the wreck to look for another miracle, another survivor. It was a hopeless task, but one of those hopeless tasks you feel compelled to pursue to the bitter end.

"Looks bad," said the doctor. We heard his prognosis through our earphones while we were trying to get inside the wreck. What we were attempting was rough because the ship's crumpled wall hung over us like a basketball over a bunch of flies.

"What's wrong with her?"

"She's still alive," said the doctor. "But we can't help her. She's a Snowmaiden."

Our doctor is inclined to couch his comparisons in poetic terms, but their transparency is not always apparent to the uninitiated. Yet the comparison of the girl to the Snowmaiden of folklore—the girl made of snow who came to life only to melt under the rays of the sun—proved to be particularly apt.

"We are accustomed," continued the doctor, "to accept water as the basis of life. She has ammonia."

The significance of his words didn't sink in at once.

"At Earth pressure," said the doctor, "ammonia boils at minus thirty-three Centigrade and freezes at minus seventy-eight."

Then everything became clear.

Since my earphones were now silent, I figured they were looking at the girl. For them she had become a phantom who would dissolve into a cloud of steam if her helmet were removed.

Navigator Bauer chose a most inappropriate time to demonstrate his erudition.

"It is theoretically predictable. The atomic weight of ammonia is seventeen; water, eighteen. Their specific heat is almost identical. Ammonia, which is as light as water, readily gives up a proton. It is an excellent solvent."

I have always envied people who, without digging into reference books, can rattle off facts that are never used. Or hardly ever.

"But at low temperatures, ammonium proteins would be too stable," objected the doctor, as if the girl were merely a theoretical construct, a model generated by Gleb Bauer's imagination.

No one replied to his objection.

We spent about an hour and a half sifting through the wrecked ship's compartments before we found a tank of an ammonium gas mixture intact. A miracle; but nowhere as great as the one that had occurred earlier.

I dropped in at the sick bay as I usually did after I came off watch. It reeked of ammonia. In fact our entire ship did. There was no way to fight the odor.

The doctor had a hacking cough. He was seated before a long row of flasks, test tubes, and tanks. Hoses and pipes protruded from some of them and disappeared into a partition. Above the porthole was a loudspeaker-translator device.

"Is she asleep?" I asked.

"No, she's asked for you already," said the doctor. His voice sounded muffled and querulous. The lower part of his face was covered by a mask. Each day he had to tackle several almost insoluble problems related to his patient's nutritional, medical, and psychological needs. His boundless pride exacerbated his querulousness. We had been flying for over two weeks, and Snowmaiden was healthy. But desperately lonely.

My eyes burned and my throat tickled. Sure, I could have improvised a mask, but it would have made me seem too squeamish. If I were in Snowmaiden's place, I would certainly be upset if my hosts approached me wearing gas masks.

The oval porthole framed Snowmaiden's face like an old-fashioned portrait.

"Hello," she said. Then, having exhausted almost her entire vocabulary, she switched on the translator. She knew I liked to hear her real voice now and then, so before turning on the translator, she would say something directly to me.

"What have you been doing?" I asked. The soundproofing was poor, so I could hear her chatter coming from behind the partition. Her lips moved, and several seconds elapsed before her words reached me through the translator, permitting me to enjoy her face and the shifting of the pupils of her eyes, which changed color like the sea on a cloudy, windy day.

"I remember what my mother taught me," said Snowmaiden in the translator's cold, expressionless voice. "I never thought I would have to prepare my own food. I thought Mother was ridiculous. But now the things she taught me have come in handy."

Snowmaiden laughed before the translator had processed her words.

"I'm learning to read now, too," she told me.

"I know. Do you remember the letter Y?"

"It's a very funny-looking letter. But F is even funnier. You know, I broke one little book."

107

Turning his face away from the stinking vapor coming from a test tube, the doctor raised his head and said, "You should have thought twice before giving her a book. At minus fifty, the plastic pages become brittle."

"That's what happened," said Snowmaiden.

When the doctor had gone, Snowmaiden and I stood there facing each other. The glass felt cold to my touch. To her it seemed almost hot. We had forty minutes alone before Bauer would return with his dictaphone and begin tormenting Snowmaiden with his endless questions: How does this function on your planet? And that? How does such-and-such reaction proceed under your conditions?

Snowmaiden would mimic Bauer amusingly and complain to me: "After all, I'm not a biologist; I could make a mistake. And later it could prove very embarrassing."

I brought her pictures and photographs of people, cities, and plants. She would laugh and question me about details that to me seemed so trivial. Then her questions would cease abruptly and she would look past me dreamily.

"What's the matter?"

"I'm lonely—and afraid."

"Don't worry. We'll get you home."

"That's not the reason."

On that particular day she asked me, "Do you have a picture of her?"

"Of whom?" I asked.

"The girl waiting for you at home."

"No one's waiting for me."

"That's not true," said Snowmaiden. She could be terribly dogmatic, especially when she didn't believe something. For example, she didn't believe in roses.

"Why don't you believe me?"

Snowmaiden didn't reply.

The cloud drifting above the sea hid the sun, and the waves changed color, turning cold and gray, but the water close to shore remained green. Snowmaiden could not conceal her mood and thoughts. When she was in good spirits, her eyes were blue, even violet. But when she was sad, they faded at once, turning gray. And anger would turn them green.

The day she opened her eyes for the first time aboard our ship, she was in pain. I shouldn't have looked at her eyes. They were black and bottomless, and we could do nothing for her until we had equipped our laboratory to fit her needs. The way we rushed to finish the job! As though the ship was about to explode. And she had remained silent. Only about three hours later were we able to transfer her to the laboratory. The doctor had remained with her and helped her remove her helmet.

The following morning her eyes had become limpid lilac pools, shining with curiosity. But they had darkened imperceptibly when they had met my gaze—

Bauer entered earlier than usual, and seemed very happy. Snowmaiden smiled at him and said, "The aquarium is at your service."

"I don't know what you mean, Snowmaiden," said Bauer.

"And your aquarium contains a fish for you to dissect."

"I would say an exotic goldfish for me to admire." Bauer isn't easily rattled.

Snowmaiden's gray-eye moods were occurring with increasing frequency. Was that so surprising for someone confined for weeks in a six-by-nine-foot chamber? Her comparison to an aquarium was very apt.

"I must be going," I said. But Snowmaiden did not respond with her usual plea to hurry back.

Her gray eyes looked at Gleb in anguish. I tried to analyze my emotional state, aware of how unrealistic it was—like falling in love with a portrait of Mary, Queen of Scots, or a statue of Nefertiti. Perhaps it was no more than pity for a lonely creature whose dependency on us had, in a surprising manner, made life pleasanter for everyone aboard. She had brought something fine into our lives which compelled us, like a boy before his first date, to smarten up our personal appearance and display greater kindness and generosity. The obvious hopelessness of my infatuation evoked in my fellow crew members a feeling midway between pity and envy, incompatible as such feelings may be. At times I wished that someone would taunt me, do something to get me angry and make me explode. But no one took such liberties. My comrades saw me as blissfully dotty, and this separated and isolated me from them.

That evening Dr. Streshny called me on the intercom. "Snowmaiden is asking for you."

"Is anything wrong?"

"Nothing. Don't worry."

I ran to the sick bay where Snowmaiden was waiting for me at the porthole.

"Sorry to bother you," she said. "But it suddenly occurred to me that if I should die I wouldn't see you again."

"Nonsense, you're not going to die," muttered the doctor.

My gaze shifted involuntarily to the dials on the equipment.

"Stay for a while," Snowmaiden said to me.

The doctor invented some excuse to leave.

"I want to touch you," said Snowmaiden. "It doesn't seem fair that I can't touch you without burning myself."

"It's easier for me," I said stupidly. "I'll only get frostbite."

"Are we almost there?"

"Yes. Four more days."

"I don't want to go home, because while I'm here I can imagine that I'm touching you. I wouldn't have you there. Lay your palm against the pane."

I obeyed.

Snowmaiden pressed her forehead against the glass, and I imagined that my fingers were penetrating the transparent mass of glass and touching her.

Snowmaiden raised her head and tried to smile. "Did you freeze your fingers?"

"We must find a neutral planet," I said.

"What kind?"

"A neutral one. In between. With a constant temperature of minus forty."

"That's too hot."

"All right, then minus forty-five. Can you take that?"

"Of course," said Snowmaiden. "But that wouldn't be any

way to live, always uncomfortable, merely tolerating our environment."

"I was only joking."

"I know you were."

"I won't be able to write to you," I said. "I'd need special paper that wouldn't crumble. And then there's that odor—"

"How does water smell? Doesn't it smell to you?" asked Snowmaiden.

"Not at all."

"How amazing!"

"There, you see, you've cheered up," I said.

"Would I fall in love with you if our blood were the same?"

"I don't know. At the beginning I fell in love with you, but then I realized we could never live together."

"Thank you."

Snowmaiden was excited on the last day, and although she told me that she couldn't imagine parting with us—with me— her thoughts darted about, flitting from one thing to another. Later, when I was packing her belongings in the laboratory, she confessed that she feared the end of the journey more than anything else. She was torn between me, whom she must leave behind, and the whole world that was waiting for her.

Her people's patrol ship had been escorting us for the past half hour, and the translator on the captain's bridge kept crackling away, processing their language with difficulty. Bauer entered the laboratory and announced that we were coming in for a landing at the spaceport. He tried to read the name of it. Snowmaiden corrected his pronunciation and then asked if he had checked her space suit thoroughly.

"I'll check it right away," said Gleb. "What are you afraid of? You've no more than thirty steps to go."

"I want to be sure I make them," said Snowmaiden, unaware that she had offended Gleb. She turned to me. "Will you check it again?" she asked.

"All right," I replied.

Gleb shrugged his shoulders and left. Three minutes later he returned and put her space suit on the table. The tanks thumped softly against the plastic, and Snowmaiden winced as if she had been struck. Then she rapped on the little door of the forward-chamber.

"Give me the space suit. I'll check it myself."

The wall that had sprung up between us crushed me; my head felt as if it were in a vise. I knew that we were parting, but that we must not part like this.

We made a soft landing. Snowmaiden was in her space suit. I thought she would leave the laboratory earlier, but she wouldn't risk it until she heard the captain's voice over the intercom: "Landing party, get into space suits. Outside temperature is minus fifty-three."

The hatch was open, and those who wished to say good-bye again to Snowmaiden waited beside it. While she spoke with the doctor, I caught up with her and went out on deck toward the ramp.

Low clouds drifted above this very strange world. A squat yellow car halted about thirty meters away, and several people stood beside it on stone slabs. They weren't wearing space suits. Why should they in their own home? The small welcoming crowd seemed lost in the vastness of the spaceport's endless field.

Another car pulled up and its passengers stepped out. I heard Snowmaiden approaching me, and turned around. The others withdrew and left us alone.

Snowmaiden wasn't looking at me. She was scanning the crowd for a familiar face. Suddenly she spied it, raised her hand, and waved. A woman separated herself from the crowd and ran along the slabs toward the ramp. Snowmaiden rushed down to meet her.

I stood there because I was the only one on the ship who hadn't said a last good-bye to Snowmaiden. Besides, I was holding a large bundle of her belongings. Finally I was included in the landing party and had to accompany Bauer for his negotiations with the spaceport authorities. We couldn't hang around here too long; we would have to depart in an hour. The woman said something to Snowmaiden, who laughed and flung off her helmet, which fell down and rolled along the slabs. Snowmaiden ran her hand through her hair. I watched as the woman pressed her cheek to Snowmaiden and thought that both of them probably felt warm. Snowmaiden said something to the woman and suddenly ran back to the ship. As she ascended the ramp she looked at me and pulled off her gloves.

"Forgive me," she said. "I didn't say good-bye to you." It wasn't her voice, but the translator above the hatch, which one of the crew had prudently switched on. But I heard her voice too.

"Take off your glove," she said. "It's only minus fifty here."

I unfastened a glove and no one stopped me, although the captain and doctor had heard and understood her words.

I didn't feel the cold, neither then, nor when she took my hand and pressed it to her cheek for an instant. I pulled back my palm, but it was too late. My hand had left a purple outline on her scorched cheek.

"It's all right," said Snowmaiden, swinging her arms to relieve the pain. "It will pass. If it doesn't, so much the better."

"Are you out of your mind?" I said.

"Put on your glove—you'll get frostbite," said Snowmaiden. She looked at me, and her dark blue, almost black eyes were completely dry.

Snowmaiden returned to the woman and they walked toward the car. When they reached it, Snowmaiden halted and raised her hand to wave good-bye to me and the rest of the crew.

The doctor turned to me. "Drop in later to see me," he said. "I'll put some salve on your hand and bandage it."

"It doesn't hurt," I assured him.

"It will later," said the doctor.

The First Layer of Memory

SUICIDES usually leave notes saying, "No one is to blame for my death." But with me it's different—you can blame the telephone for all my troubles. It's my enemy and I'm its slave. Anyone with guts in a situation like mine would have ripped out the wires and smashed it to pieces. On the other hand, what would we do for martyrs if everyone cut up for firewood the cross he was supposed to bear? Anytime anyone wants something from me, he picks up the phone. If he had to come over on foot or take a bus, he'd think twice before coming. If you're the owner of a telephone, you know what I mean. If you're not, you don't.

I had barely dragged myself home that day. It was spring, and deceptively hot, bound to hit near-freezing temperatures during the night. And it did. So there I am in bed, nice and cozy, with an Agatha Christie that I borrowed for two days, when the phone starts ringing at eleven-thirty. I let the damned thing ring about ten times, hoping it would ring itself out. But it didn't. Shivering, I picked up the receiver and growled something indistinct into it, something that could be interpreted by the hearer according to his pleasure.

"Givi"—it was David's voice—"I didn't wake you, did I?"

"You sure did."

"I thought so." He didn't even bother to apologize. "Listen, our car is on its way over for you. Right now. The boss's already at the institute."

"I'm very touched by his devotion," I confessed. "But what the hell is our esteemed chief doing there at this ungodly hour? Some juvenile delinquents break in to steal parts for their erector sets?"

"Stop clowning, Givi. I'm dead serious. The car will be at your place any minute. It's picking up Rusiko, too. How far is her place?"

"Practically next door. As a matter of fact, I took her home tonight and it looked like her old man was aiming at me from the balcony with a shotgun."

David hung up on me, which meant he was dead serious. I decided that I wasn't going anywhere, but began to dress, just in case. I was getting into my jacket when I heard a car honking under the window. It sounded like the director's.

It was as cold as hell. Rusiko was sitting in the black Volga without her makeup. She certainly acted like hot stuff. After all, how often are limousines sent out to pick up ordinary surgical nurses?

"Rusiko," I said as I slid in beside her, "what's it all about?"

"I haven't the slightest." She made it sound as though she was in the know but had to wait to make sure that I had clearance for such a vital secret. "I got a phone call. David called."

"Quite an honor. And what did you do to deserve it?"

Rusiko shrugged her shoulders.

"Come on, now; what did he say to you? After all, what official or moral right does he have to get such a beautiful young woman out of bed at this time of night?"

"Emergency operation. On account of the earthquake, I guess."

"What earthquake?"

"There was an earthquake this morning," the driver said. "Somewhere up in the mountains."

"No one tells me a damned thing. When I crawled out of the lab I didn't hear a blessed word about it. You *know* that fires and earthquakes turn me on. Especially when there's a volcanic eruption in my hometown."

"There aren't any volcanoes here," Rusiko explained. "They're all on Kamchatka."

"Thanks for setting me straight."

We pulled up in front of the institute. It was a madhouse. You would have thought it was quitting time. There were cars all over the place, people were running around, and lights were still burning in half the windows.

"Looks like the earth is still quaking," I said, sliding out the door. And I must admit that all sorts of premonitions came over me.

David and Lordkipanidze himself were standing in the middle of the lobby.

"Always at your post," I greeted them, dispensing with hellos, since I had already had the honor of paying my respects to both my colleagues that morning.

"Ah, here's Givi, too," said Lord. He turned to Rusiko. "Upstairs to the operating room, right away. I'll be there soon."

"Pardon me, my friend," I said, "would you mind telling me where I can find the information desk? I'd like to get a sneak preview of my near future."

"Tell him what's up," Lord shot to David as he hoisted his bulky frame up the stairs.

"OK, in a couple of words," David warned me, as if more than four words and a comma would be too much for me to swallow at one stretch. "Pachuliya phoned me. He's on the first-aid squad. You know him, don't you?"

"Get to the point. You were told to fill me in, not to clarify my personal relationship to Pachuliya."

"Right. Of course." David fiddled with his glasses. "They have a patient in deep shock, and they don't know yet if they can pull him out of it. The epicenter of the earthquake was right there in the mountains. Fortunately, it was a small one." David unconsciously pinched the air to show the size.

"Impossible! They don't make them that small!"

"Well, they say dishes were hopping around in their cupboards in some sections of Tbilisi."

"Probably from heavy traffic. Besides, where do we come in? We're no first-aid squad. We're strictly a research outfit. The Brain Research Center."

"That's just the point. We're the Brain Research Center. Pachuliya knew what we were working on. He attended a conference in Kiev in February where Lord delivered a paper. So he remembered it. Of course the idea is wild, but lives depend on it."

David's attention was suddenly diverted. A charming, slender young lady dashed into the lobby and rushed toward us in confusion.

"Where is he? Is he alive?" she whispered.

The girl was so deeply distressed that even an inveterate egotist and cynic like myself turned away without saying a word. I never know what to say in such situations, but David has a great bedside manner.

"Pardon me, miss, but who were you asking about?"

"Beso. Beso Guramishvili."

"Ah, yes, of course," said David. "I must tell you frankly that his condition is serious, but certainly not hopeless."

"May I see him?"

"Not at the moment. Tomorrow."

"You're not lying to me, are you?" the girl asked.

"Why should I lie? Beso is asleep now and mustn't be disturbed. I suggest that you come tomorrow morning and then—"

"He was hurt badly, wasn't he? In the cave?"

"No," said David, "he was found outside—on the road."

"What about the others?"

"They're searching for them."

"How come he got out and the others didn't?"

David decided to put it to her squarely.

"Now listen to me. Beso was found two hours ago on a road forty miles from the city. A truck driver coming from Tbilisi found him and was going to take him to the regional hospital. But while he was trying to help Beso, the mountain patrol arrived and recognized Beso. They didn't touch him until the first-aid squad came from the city. Do you understand now?"

I said that I was still as confused as ever, and it was obvious the girl was still confused, too.

David was taken aback. "What don't you understand?" he asked me.

"Why would the mountain patrol be looking for Beso? Is he a mountain climber?"

"No, a speleologist. *You* wouldn't have read about him—all you read is junk. Last year speleologists began exploring a cave forty miles from here. There were articles about it everywhere. It was a big expedition."

"Eighteen people," said the girl. She was a little calmer now. "They began last year and mapped out eight miles. You can't imagine how fascinating it is there. Last fall Beso took me with him as far as their base camp. What a fantastic stalactitic cavern there—" She broke off abruptly. "Alyosha!" she shouted.

She had spotted a husky, red-bearded chap in a stormcoat, one of those tiresome types who always seem to have their noses in the most unlikely places. The girl rushed toward him.

David elucidated. "A rescue worker."

"So let's hear the rest," I said. "Where do we come into the picture?"

"Beso was one of the speleologists. It was the second week the group was working underground. They had a doctor with them and maintained radio contact with the surface—a monitoring squad was stationed aboveground. This afternoon there was an earthquake. The cave entrance got blocked up, contact was broken, and no one knows what happened to the speleologists. Picture this: the rescue workers are trying to bore through the blockage; they search for other entrances to the cave, and lo and behold—Beso Guramishvili turns up on the road, ten miles from the main entrance."

"And he can't tell you anything."

"Right—he can't tell us anything. And there's every reason to believe that they won't be able to bring him around today."

"Is the entrance solidly blocked?"

"Seems to be. Ask Alyosha. He brought Beso here. He's a friend of his."

"Ask him yourself. You don't need my help for that."

"They might need help from both of us," David said.

"What do you mean?"

"The machine."

"How can that help them reach the speleologists?"

"Let's go upstairs. Think about it on the way, Givi. Maybe you can guess."

I started upstairs. I couldn't figure out how the machine could dig out the speleologists.

"Listen, David, couldn't this Beso guy have made it to the surface before the entrance got blocked?"

"Impossible. He was in there with the rest of them."

"Suppose he was hurled to the surface somehow?"

"Come on, be sensible."

"So you mean he got out after the earthquake?"

"Right."

We walked up to Lord's office. He was talking with a stranger in a white smock.

"I get it," I said. "Beso knows how to get to the others without having to break through the blocked entrance."

"You're practically a genius. That's precisely what Pachuliya thought of when he was bringing Beso to Tbilisi in the ambulance."

We stood in the doorway of Lord's office, but he ignored us.

"Guramishvili is ranked as a first-rate mountain climber," the

119

stranger was saying to Lord. "He ranks among the top ten in the republic. Which means, if there was a chance that anyone could reach some inaccessible outlet, Beso would be your man. There was no one else in the group like him. But he won't talk."

The way he said it, you'd think Beso was deliberately holding out to spite him.

"So, my dear colleagues," Lord addressed us, "Comrade Kiknadze believes we can help him."

"We must find out how to get to the speleologists," continued Lord, after a brief pause. "Apparently we're the only ones who can."

David asked, "Should we get the setup ready?"

"I've already ordered it," said Lord. "What I want to know is, who is going to be the recipient?"

"I am," replied David.

Lord looked at him very skeptically. I knew what he was thinking.

David comes from a good family. His parents fed him lavishly and discouraged him from taking part in sports, so he ended up soft, warm, and plump—but to his family's surprise, a real worker. He's near-sighted, and his parents took him to eye doctors in Moscow, Leningrad, and maybe even Vladivostok. Anybody else would have developed an intense dislike for medicine, but he's in love with it. A masochist.

"If it works, you might have to go in," Lord told David.

Then he turned to me.

I involuntarily straightened up. We Georgians are theoretically long-lived, but all my aunts and uncles managed to die young, or at least before they could collect their pensions. They were killed in wars, fell from cliffs—one traveled two thousand miles to get himself drowned in the Atlantic Ocean. Now it seemed that I too was to meet a premature death, and no one except me had any second thoughts about it.

"Well, how about it?" Lord asked.

"Let's get to work," I said.

David mumbled something about his experience and willingness, but Lord was already on his way to the laboratory.

"David," I tried to console him, "to each his own, as the Greeks used to say."

"Romans," he corrected me.

"To each his own," I repeated as I left him. "Some must work with their heads and some must do the legwork."

I love our machine, probably because my love for it pays off in cash and occasional bonuses. It's like a dame—unpredictable and capricious. It occupies the basement and half of the second floor, and one minute it feeds you some startling information, the next it refuses to cooperate with you. The engineers built the machine, and we developed practical applications. But we're always unhappy with each other. They treat us medics like second-class citizens who have nothing better to do than ruin their inventions.

Recently the operating room was remodeled and faced with blue tile. Only the wall to the right of the door, occupied by a control panel, was left untiled. After all these improvements I've thought the operating room had much in common with a hotel lavatory, especially when the air conditioner is on the blink. And it's common knowledge that air conditioners conk out only in sizzling weather.

I glanced into the operating room through the glass door. Rusiko was preparing the instruments. She looked striking in her yellow smock, and when she raised her head and smiled at me, I mimed my enthusiasm for her irresistible beauty. But once again she didn't catch on.

I went to shave my head. I've finally reconciled myself to the weekly shave I must endure, and console myself with the thought that after each shave I'm a pretty close ringer for a certain poet who had a head like a billiard ball. My friends think this shaving routine is a quirk of mine, my way of struggling against my intellectual inferiority complex. Most of my friends are intellectuals, which means they don't understand a damned thing about life.

As I shaved I recalled the first time, some two years ago, that we switched on the machine. Ruslan and another dog—a little

121

chestnut-colored circus dog whose name escapes me—were tied down to tables in the operating room. The room was white then, the ceiling leaked, and it had pretty designs on it. (I found out about the designs later, when I got to lie on one of those tables.) I had introduced the needle into Ruslan's brain, and Natella secured the monitor. Lord was worried, so he snapped at us and snarled at Rusiko. David and the engineers fussed around the console, and although the chief engineer signaled us ten minutes later that the tape had been transmitted, we still weren't sure how it would turn out.

When the dogs woke up we watched them the way jealous husbands watch their wives. The dogs lapped up milk and devoured meat, then Ruslan stared vacantly at the circus dog's trainer.

We had deliberately selected a circus dog because of its varied experiences and because it could do many more things than an ordinary mutt like Ruslan. The trainer grumbled. He didn't believe that memory could be recorded, that all the circus dog's skills and knowledge could be recorded and transferred to Ruslan. We weren't too confident about it either, and that was really rotten, because a helluva lot of money and time had been squandered on this business. And all those years many serious people considered Lord a charlatan; his engineer-friends, charlatans; and David, myself, and the other small fry, plain idiots. When, toward evening of that same day, the skeptical trainer began to issue orders to Ruslan, our precious mutt assumed a professional stance. He pranced around on his hind legs, did a perky somersault, and leaped clumsily through a paper hoop. The circus dog stared at him wide-eyed, prompting him in some sort of canine lingo. Although it went against Ruslan's grain to engage in activities beneath the dignity of a respectable dog, he went through the whole routine because his memory now contained knowledge transmitted to him from the circus dog. But after two days he forgot everything; he had returned to his normal tail-wagging, cat-chasing existence.

Utterly unconvinced that a dog could learn in five minutes what normally took months of exhaustive training, the trainer took his shaven dog, settled accounts with the bookkeeper, and departed disgruntledly. But we, on the other hand, arranged a big feast at Lord's summer cottage and sang each other's praises with toasts and speeches. Three months later I was stretched out on the operating table as a guinea pig, and since then I've been going about with a closely cropped head and trying to conceal the scars above my right ear.

That doesn't mean it's been an easy road to the top. Falling, stumbling, losing our way, we plodded on toward success; repeatedly we returned to our starting point, demoralized by the thought that we'd never find our way out of the maze. We worked with the smartest dogs in the Republic of Georgia, and for some reason they transferred to their recipients only fragments of stupid memories or the technique of biting on the sly. We also used pampered macaques and marmosets, but they couldn't absorb from their informants even the simple art of flinging banana skins at their detested keepers. Finally, we sacrificed ourselves, and for two days straight I was tormented by David's childhood guilt over having stolen a cufflink from his uncle.

The results of our experiments were incomplete; memory transmission was unreliable.

But now Natella was asking, "Givi, are you ready? The patient is here." I followed her toward the operating room. In the corridor we met Kiknadze. "Good luck!" he said to me. "This is the most important operation you have ever participated in."

"Thanks a lot," I said politely. "How nice of you to say that."

Kiknadze stiffened, trying to determine whether or not to be offended.

"Givi, why do you talk like that to people?" Natella wanted me to be as talented and as serious as Lord, and an altruist to boot. With her feminine shortsightedness she couldn't understand that if I ever succeeded in meeting the conditions for her approval she'd lose all interest in me. "You can't imagine what he's going through," she went on. "And don't forget about the relatives of those speleologists. Everyone is making demands on him."

"But I haven't asked him for anything. All I ask is to be left in peace. You know how important it is for me to be relaxed and calm before a transfer operation."

"OK, I'll relax you," said Natella.

"Never mind. David will do it. Don't deprive him of the pleasure. Besides, if you do it, I won't be in any state to receive. I'd be thinking only of you. By the way, how would you like to be my informant some time? I'll buy you a gorgeous wig afterward."

"No way," said Natella. "And not because I'm afraid of giving up my hair."

"Afraid I'll find out how you really feel about me?"

"Yes, I am."

"You flatter me."

"On the contrary."

When I appeared in the operating room, smelling sweetly of iodine, everything was ready. I went over to the table where Beso Guramishvili was lying. I realized they were doing everything in their power to keep him alive. I liked Beso: with his shaven head, he looked just like me. Or the famous poet. Only younger.

I nodded to Pachuliya. It was he who had brought Beso here. He was a fine surgeon and had been a classmate of mine, even though I hadn't admitted it to David. Pachuliya had been a straight-A student and used to give me inspirational advice.

"Givi, are you ready?" asked Lord in a fatherly tone, sounding as if he were inviting me to take a stroll or accompany him to an ice cream parlor.

I tried to relax, using autosuggestion. First the muscles in my forehead loosened up, then my eye muscles.

If I turned my head as I lay on the table, I could see Beso's sharp, swarthy profile. The anesthesiologists had arrived at a decision, and a very young cardiologist from our institute was permitted to join their lofty deliberations. I tried to imagine what it was like there, in the cave. Probably very dark and frightening.

"I hope Beso never stole cufflinks from his uncle," I said to

David. And those were my last words before the anesthetic knocked me out.

When I came to, it took me a while to figure out who I was and where I was. When I finally fit the pieces together, I went back to sleep, because I was afraid I'd be asked questions that I couldn't answer. It's rotten when something's expected of you and you can't produce. If you've ever flunked an exam you know what I mean.

When I woke up again, I was in my hospital room. A light was burning behind the frosted glass, and human silhouettes floated along the glass like pantomime shadows. As usual, I had a miserable headache, but worse than that was my sense of personal failure. Lord had counted on me, and I hadn't come through with the goods.

I raised my hand to look at my watch, but, of course, it wasn't there. Voices rustled behind the door. My hearing was keener now, and I made out someone's low voice, probably Lord's.

"According to our test results, it takes two or three hours before the new memory begins to take root."

The door opened and Natella tiptoed in. I didn't care to talk with anyone, so I closed my eyes. Natella fussed around the little table by my bedside and a glass jingled. After she left I heard her voice in the corridor.

"He's still asleep."

"Coffee's ready." That was Rusiko's voice.

The flitting shadows on the glass panels vanished. I was grateful to Rusiko for figuring out how to divert them from my door. Apparently, they were just as happy to leave me alone.

Something was nagging at my brain. I had forgotten something. Something important. I saw Beso lying in the next bed and it struck me that I had never before seen myself from the outside. Really, not myself but himself. Still, there was something I had failed to do but should have done, although this commitment was really Beso's, not mine. I was worried that I had lost this *something*. Somewhere, in the depths of my consciousness, I was still myself, and I realized that Beso's thoughts were beginning to take root. But what was this *something* that eluded me? Was it about the cave? No, not that. I realized that *it* was more important right now than the cave. I, me, knew nothing about the cave. I couldn't remember it because I'd never been there or anywhere near it. Whatever it was that had eluded me must be in the pocket of Beso's jeans.

Then, without Beso, I had to work out my own thoughts, thoughts that disturbed only me, that pursued me alone. Beso didn't know where the jeans were. He knew nothing about the institute where he was now hospitalized. But I did.

Outside my door it was quiet. Only a few minutes had passed, and Lord and the others obviously were still busy drinking coffee and discussing whether the memory transfer had been successful. They wanted to find a way into the cave and I knew nothing about it. That elusive *something* meant nothing to them. But it did to me. To me and who else? Who else? Ah, yes, Rezo. To Rezo, because I had promised him—

When Beso was brought to the institute, he was undressed, and his clothing sent to the storeroom on the first floor. I knew that I must get into the storeroom and find those jeans.

Now, right now, I, Givi, must assert myself and press the call button. Natella would respond immediately, and Lord, too, and I would tell them about the jeans and what must be removed from them. But somehow I couldn't do it. I must go to the storeroom myself. But it will be dangerous to leave through the door because Natella might return at any moment. I will have to lower myself from the second floor. Not a very clever thing to do. Impetuous as I may be, I must get a grip on myself and keep in mind that I am primarily a scientist, and only secondarily a repository for Beso's recollections.

I sat on the edge of the bed for a moment, trying to shake off the nausea and dizziness. Suddenly I realized that my attire consisted solely of shorts. My dear friends had forgotten to clothe me, even in a pair of hospital pajamas.

I went to the window and opened it. Just as in an adventure story, it creaked loud enough to awaken the dead. A dark flower bed lay far below. Maybe they had made a mistake and had put me on the tenth floor? I stood there, hesitating. It was bitter cold.

Suddenly my sense of me, Givi, vanished. I must hurry to retrieve that *something* and do what I had to do. Footsteps in the corridor. Perhaps Natella had sensed that something was wrong and was on her way to my room to investigate. I threw my legs over the windowsill, pushed myself away from the wall, and jumped. My feet struck the ground; I lost my balance and fell on my side. Though I was dirtied, I didn't feel any pain, only annoyance with myself for my clumsiness. Beso would have done better.

I sat in the flower bed and listened. Was it my room that someone had entered? If it was Natella, all hell would break loose and I'd never make it to the storeroom. But everything was quiet. I rose, shook the dirt from my knees, and hugged the wall as I made my way toward the service entrance.

With the moon shining on me, I stood out against the white wall like a beetle on a piece of paper. Ah, there's the window. It's covered by bars and inaccessible to the uninitiated. But only yesterday I had overheard the custodian complaining about the lock being defective and knew that the institute's locksmith planned to put in a new one. Hopefully he had obliged us by removing the old one and hadn't yet installed a new one.

After I entered through the service door, I realized I was chilled to the bone. I stood there for about half a minute inhaling the warm air in the dark corridor; then I groped around until I found the storeroom door, and pushed it. It opened obediently. Assuming that the institute had no time to worry about burglars tonight, I switched on the light. Beso's clothes lay on the table. When he was brought in, the custodian was out, so his clothes were simply piled here. My instantaneous recognition of Beso's things came as no great surprise; it would have been more surprising if I hadn't recognized them.

I was freezing; besides, I didn't want to be discovered here in my half-naked state. I pulled on the damp jeans, which turned out to be about my size, put on a T-shirt and a well-worn sweater. Everything was dirty and one sleeve of the sweater had dried blood on it. I found Beso's shoes under the table, but they were too small—a complication that neither Beso nor I had anticipated. I opened the wardrobe containing patients' property and selected a pair of shoes. They were shiny patent leather, incompatible with the rest of my attire, but they didn't pinch. From the pocket of my jeans I took out a small plastic packet. Inside the plastic wrapping was a pouch made from newspaper.

"Rezo handed me a packet. In the light of our one remaining lantern, his face seemed more emaciated than usual. The light shone from above, turning his eyes into two black holes. 'Will you promise to do it?' asked Rezo. 'I promise,' I said."

Although Rezo was a stranger to me, this picture flashed vividly through my consciousness. I stood there, hesitating.

"Now what?" I asked Beso mentally. "Should we go back? They're going to notice we're gone."

Suddenly I realized where I must go. And fast, too. To the village of Mokvi. A bus could take me there. From the depot. I took my watch from the table. Beso's. It was still running. Four-twenty, it said. Less than three hours had passed since the operation.

I must not delay another minute. Turning off the light, I left the storeroom. Public transportation was still asleep and dreaming, but the bus station was relatively near. Maybe I could catch a cab. That would do it. I crossed the lawn to the institute's gates as fast as I could. The farther away I could get in the next few minutes, the better it would be for me, for Beso, and for—for whom?

"You'll recognize the house. The last one on the street. Surrounded by wild grapevines. Roses in front of it. No one in the village has so many."

It was Rezo's voice.

I passed through the half-opened gates. The institute was a madhouse now, so all the rules were ignored. I wondered where the night watchman could be.

The Kura River murmured nearby. A dog barked. The dogs confined in the institute's basement replied. I thought I heard a shout coming from the direction of the institute. Were they calling me? I walked along the highway toward the city. I would have run but I was afraid of getting dizzy and nauseous again. I turned around. The green light of a cab leaped out from behind a bend. Moving to the middle of the road, I raised my hand. The cab stopped.

"Can't you see I'm off duty?" asked the driver, thrusting his head out the window. "I'm not picking up passengers."

"Please, just to the bus station."

"It's out of my way."

"OK, how much?"

"You don't have that kind of money."

"It's urgent. Please take me."

We settled on three rubles. The driver had surrendered to the power of cold cash, but he was still irritated.

"A rock tore loose from under my feet, and a blast of air struck my face. The air was dense, and it swallowed up the sound of the cave-in. I fell down on the ground and struck myself painfully on someone's helmet. I didn't think I could die. I wished the rumbling would end quickly so I could make my way to the surface. But it continued, as if rocks were trying to fill up every gap in the mountain."

"We're here," said the cabby. "Now I'll have to go an extra ten miles. Pay up."

I froze. My hands didn't know where to look for money. It was in Givi's sport coat, and I was wearing Beso's jeans and sweater. Not a kopek in them.

"I forgot my wallet," I replied calmly, because I was at the depot now and it was less than an hour's ride to Mokvi.

"The hell you say," exclaimed the driver. "You've got to be kidding!"

"Come to the institute tomorrow. I'll give you ten rubles."

"You're kidding," he repeated, with even greater conviction. "You're going to pay for your jokes, buddy. Come on, we're going to have a nice little chat at the police station."

He reached across me and closed the door.

"Take something as security," I urged.

129

"What can I take from you?" he asked, looking me over. "What the hell can a person take from someone like you?"

He had lost all faith in humanity.

I remembered. "My watch. Here, take my watch."

I didn't wait for his reply. I tugged at the strap and handed him the watch.

"I don't need your damned watch," he said angrily.

"A Seiko is a very fine watch," I said placatingly. It belonged to Beso, so I knew it was a Seiko.

That seemed to do the trick.

"OK," he said. "I suppose anything is possible. Just don't forget my number."

He told me his number but I didn't have time to write it down, for an early bus was pulling up to the waiting room. I ran toward it. The route number above the windshield told me it was headed in the opposite direction.

The cab driver ran after me. "Hey, don't forget my number!" he shouted.

"I won't," I called out and hurried to the waiting room.

It was still night in the waiting room. A few stray passengers dozed on benches, whiling away the time. I burst in and began to hunt around wildly for a timetable. Finally I spotted the board and rushed up to it. I had never been to Mokvi, but Beso had. It had been a long time ago, but he'd been there. The next bus for Mokvi was leaving in an hour and a half.

I stood in front of the board. My last valuable, Beso's watch, was gone. I'd have to walk along the highway and catch a lift with a passing truck. But I still had to get to the highway.

Ah, a familiar-looking face. The girl over there, asleep, with her head resting on the back of the bench. It was the same girl who had rushed into the institute and inquired about Beso. What the hell am I saying! That's my sister Nana. She was probably chased out of the institute and told not to return before eight. Maybe she's going to see Mother. Mother still doesn't know about the accident.

I took a step toward Nana, hoping to comfort her, to tell her that everything was all right with me, Beso.

Nana raised her head, as if I had called out to her. She stared straight at me, and I was afraid she'd recognize Beso's sweater and jeans. I took one step back; I could see she was trying to place me. After all, she had seen me quite recently, but at the institute I had been dressed respectably in a suit and tie. She kept staring at me, and I heard heavy footsteps approaching from behind.

I knew they were coming toward me. I swung around sharply, ready for flight. The cab driver was striding through the waiting room, the Seiko dangling from his index finger.

I was afraid that Nana would recognize the watch, so I walked over to the cabby to block off her view.

"You didn't write down my number," he said.

"Let's go," I said, trying to angle him away from Nana. "We'll talk outside."

He followed me out. It was chilly. Beso's sweater offered scant protection against the icy wind blowing down on us. I hunched up.

"Where do you have to go?" asked the cabby.

"To Mokvi."

"Yeah, I know the place. My brother used to live there. Before the war. Got married and stayed there a while. Then moved to Telavi. Do you have a girl friend there?"

"Why?"

"You seem mighty upset about something." He took out a pack of cigarettes and offered me one.

"Thanks, I don't smoke."

"Don't get me wrong. I'm not chasing after you for those three rubles. I finished working an hour ago. I don't like chiselers."

I told him the simple truth. "My wallet's in my other pants."

I looked around the square, hoping for a miracle, for a bus with a sign above its windshield reading "Mokvi."

"What's the big deal in Mokvi?" asked the cabby.

"Look, you've finished working and I'm broke."

"Keep your nose out of my business. You don't have to tell me what to do. Get in the car."

"What?"

"I told you to get in! I'm not going to wait here all night for you."

We drove out of the city. It was already getting light. The warm, cozy cab made me drowsy.

"So you think I'm nuts, eh?" asked the cabby.

"No, I think you're a very kind person."

"Me kind? I've got your watch as security anyway."

The traffic light turned red. We stood at the deserted crossing for what seemed like ages. It was as though the light didn't want to change.

"What time is it?" I asked.

"You're still not getting your watch back. It's five-thirty. Are you late?"

"Yes."

"Which house in Mokvi do you want. I know them all."

I didn't reply. I had forgotten which house I wanted. I trusted Beso.

"I couldn't see Rezo's eyes. The light came from above. The doctor was groaning nearby. What a time for a doctor to break a leg! . . . You'll recognize his house at once. . . ."

"The last house on the street," I said. "It's covered with grapevines. And roses. No one in Mokvi has so many roses."

"I'd say so, too. Bagrat, the cripple, lives there. Are you going to see him?"

"I don't know. I haven't been there for a long time. He used to live alone. His son works in Tbilisi."

"I promised my father that I'd try to find it," said Rezo. "I think it's a lot of nonsense, but he believes in it. I brought a specialist to examine him, but the specialist doubted that anything could be done for him. My father is old. But he believes in it; says the old-timers did, too. They knew the way to the cave."

I drew the plastic packet from my pocket and opened the newspaper pouch. Bits of golden resin, like amber, lay in the paper. They felt soapy and light and gave off a waxy, sweet fragrance.

132

"What's that?" asked the driver. "Do you raise bees?"

"No, it's medicine."

He slammed on the brakes. I barely kept the resin from spilling. He pulled over onto the shoulder.

"Listen," he asked, "where did you find that stuff?"

"In a cave."

"Right!" The driver was delighted. "Why did you keep your mouth shut? You've found mountain balsam. The stuff that cures all diseases?"

"The old people believe in it."

"You're Pop Bagrat's son? Why didn't you say so?"

"I'm not his son. His son asked me to deliver this to him."

"When my mother was dying she asked me to get her some. Where can you get it these days? The doctors don't believe in it. Hasn't been tested, they say."

"Do you need it?" I asked.

"What for? I'm healthy. Do you really think it does any good? Our district doctor told me there was something to the old ways of practicing medicine. What do you think?"

"I don't know. It's very important for a patient to have faith in the medicine he's taking."

"Right you are. Aspirin—that's my cure-all."

We swerved back onto the highway again, and after going about two miles, turned off on a country road. A blue arrow on a sign pointed to MOKVI—4.

The old house *was* covered by grapevines. Rosebushes behind the house enjoyed the cool of the dawn. The roses hadn't bloomed yet; it was too early. A puppy sporting a torn ear dashed to the gate to greet us.

"Thanks," I said to the driver. "I've got your number in my head, so don't worry. I'll find you tomorrow."

"I'm off tomorrow," said the driver. Suddenly he shoved the watch into my hand. "Here, take it. You should have told me at the beginning what it was all about."

"Hold onto the watch."

"Forget it. Do you think I drove you all the way out here for a few lousy rubles?"

133

I took the watch.

"If you'd like, I'll split the balsam with you."

"What do I need it for? My mother's dead now, and I'm healthy."

"Maybe it'll come in handy sometime."

"Nope. Aspirin is my cure-all. You'd better hurry, young fellow. Pop Bagrat is probably waiting for you."

I pushed the gate open. The puppy moved aside politely and ran ahead of me toward the porch. The grapevines, arching above the path like a tunnel, compelled me to bend over.

"I heard Teimur's voice in the pitch dark: 'Who has an emergency lantern?' An instant before the cave-in, we were seated at a long stone table, waiting for the doctor, whose turn it was to serve the soup. We had just washed up in an underground stream and piled our helmets and rubber suits in a corner beside the walkie-talkie. We were exhausted because that day we had covered half a mile and passed through a treacherous cavern. Sitting at the long table, we were in high spirits because everything had turned out so well and only one more chamber remained to be explored, probably a small one. Tomorrow we would look for an approach to it. Then the cave-in hit. Dense, cold air struck my face. . . ."

I halted on the porch. It was quiet inside. From here you could see the village running down toward the river and a herd of cattle scattered along the slope's bright green young grass. There was a smell of smoke in the air. The little river was covered by a haze. A bullock cart creaked along the street. It was now quite light.

A little old lady, who was wearing a long black skirt that reached to the ground and a kerchief that covered her forehead, peeked out the door. She was holding a bucket.

I greeted her.

"Are you looking for Bagrat, young man?" asked the old lady, not in the least surprised by such an early visit. "He's up."

Bagrat proved to be a powerfully built old man. The wide old bed with its shiny balls on the bed posts seemed too confining for him. Apparently Bagrat had been ill for a long time. He was withered, and the skin on his cheeks and forehead seemed very dark, particularly in contrast to his yellowish beard and long locks of white hair. But his eyes had retained their clear blue color. He raised a broad, bony palm that seemed to be carved out of old wood.

"What happened to Rezo?" he asked.

He looked at me strangely, as if I were far, far away on a mountain slope; as if I were a messenger of bad tidings. The old man had steeled himself in advance for still another of those blows which a long life lavishes so generously, but it was clear that he had no intention of submitting to fate.

"Sit down," he said before I had a chance to reply.

"Rezo is alive and well," I said.

"Sit down," he repeated. I don't think he believed me.

"Rezo is alive. He sends his regards and is worried about your health."

"When did you see him?"

"Yesterday."

"Morning?"

"Afternoon."

"I had a bad premonition yesterday morning," said the old man. "Where did you see him?"

"In the cave. We're working there. With the expedition."

"That's right. In the cave. And you say nothing happened?"

I couldn't lie to him. "There was a cave-in. But we managed to dodge it. Everyone is alive."

"Why didn't Rezo come himself?"

"He stayed there to work."

"Why are you so dirty? What happened to your head? Are you tired?"

The old lady brought a tray of sliced cheese, bread, and a cut-glass decanter of white wine.

"Move the table over here," the old man ordered me. "We'll have breakfast."

I obeyed.

"What's your name?" he asked as he filled the wineglasses.

"Givi."

"I don't know any Givi among my Rezo's friends."

"I'm a newcomer to the expedition."

"You're lying." The old man was not annoyed; he was simply pointing out a fact.

"Rezo asked me to bring you some mountain balsam. He couldn't come today and it was on my way."

I removed the newspaper wrapping and handed him the bits of resin.

"Thank you, young fellow." He sniffed one of the resin lumps. "This is real mountain balsam. Rezo has been trying to find some for me for more than a year. Thank you for taking the time to bring medicine to an old man. When you're old and learn how helpless doctors are, you too will have to believe in the old remedies. When you see Rezo, tell him that his father thanks him and that I will try to get on my feet again before he returns. Will he be coming back soon?"

I realized that Givi wouldn't have been able to resist the chance to puncture the solemnity of the moment. Of course, I was still Givi. Or was it Beso?

"He'll probably be here earlier than expected. Maybe in a day or two."

I realized instantly that I shouldn't have said that. The old man knew better than I did that Rezo had to work underground at least another two weeks. I should have noticed earlier the wall calendar hanging above his head. April was circled in red pencil, and the numbers from April the second until today had been crossed out. The old man was counting the days.

So I told him everything. Almost everything. I told him that the expedition was trapped underground. We were sure that everyone was alive, but one man who had made it to the surface was ill, too ill to tell us how to get to the others. He was in the hospital where I worked and he had asked me to deliver the balsam.

The old man listened without interrupting. He closed his eyes and remained motionless; he seemed to be scarcely breathing.

"I know the entrance they used to get into the cave," he said when I had finished my story. "Many years ago, people used to look for mountain balsam in the cave. Later on they lost the trail, forgot about it. How far did the explorers get this year? Where did Beso leave them?"

I visualized the cave as it had been traced on Teimur's map. I remembered the map well, with the sections explored last year traced in India ink, the penciled twists and bends tracing this year's explorations, and the dotted lines representing future ones.

When the cave-in struck they were at their base, in the chamber containing the walkie-talkie, two miles from the main entrance. The cave-in had hit the part of the chamber where their equipment lay. Apparently when they found a lamp and inspected the damage, they saw they couldn't get through to the exit.

"You say that no one was hurt?"

"The doctor broke her arm, and another woman hurt herself badly."

"I always told Rezo that women had no place under-ground."

"The rest got off with just a few scratches. Then everyone assembled in the next chamber, and Teimur sent Beso and another man to look for a passage to the surface. They were given a lamp and started out."

"In which direction?"

I tried to remember. I visualized the passage narrowing to the size of a rabbit burrow, where you had to practically squeeze your body into the rock and didn't know whether the passage would broaden out or whether you'd be forced to crawl back.

"He went toward the east."

"Did they go very far?"

"No, they returned for an aqualung. That's a—"

"I know what it is."

"The passage widened, leading into another chamber. But the exit was under water."

"Beso went on alone?"

"Yes. They had only one aqualung left. Besides, they

137

couldn't drag the doctor and the other woman through it. Beso was a mountain climber. And skinny. Everyone was counting on him."

"What did Rezo say when they parted?"

"Rezo told him that he must find you when he got to the surface and give you the packet of balsam. He told him how to find your house."

"Why did you tell me your name was Givi and that you worked in the hospital? Were you actually at the cave? And made it to the surface?"

"I swear I've told you the truth. Beso is in the hospital."

"You seem to be an honest man, but for some reason, you keep telling lies. If you're Beso, why did you come here? Why aren't you leading a rescue team to the cave-in? If you're Givi, then how did Beso remember what happened underground yet did not say where he came out?"

"He's very ill. He forgot."

The old man sighed. He was tired of challenging me.

"Listen to me, now," he said, "if you go uphill from the village along the ravine for two miles, you'll see an opening in the ground. I myself have never gone through it. If you go in the direction you said Beso was coming from, you can get to the people trapped down there. How far had Beso gone?"

"He was found on the road late at night. Around ten o'clock."

"Where?"

"I told you where."

"No, that's far from that place, but you can try it anyway. I'll send Georgi with you. He's a smart fellow and knows those places."

Footsteps rustled behind the door and the porch boards creaked. The old man smiled faintly.

"She's on her way already," he said. "She was listening."

"I leaped from the icy stream. I was afraid my heart would stop. I had only an aqualung, no rubber suit—it had been buried by the cave-in. I removed the aqualung and hopped around to warm myself. Compared to the water, the air seemed warm. I wondered how they were doing back there

in the cave without a lamp. When I left, they were singing. Never mind, I'll make it to the surface and warm myself up there. I checked the compass for water. It was dry. I chose a passage that led above the others, to the east. . . ."

The porch boards creaked sharply. A short fellow in army pants and a blue shirt stood in the doorway.

"Did you send for me, Pop?"

"Good morning, Georgi. I need your help, so wake up!"

Georgi rubbed his sleepy eyes.

"Can you take our guest to the crack in the upper ravine?"

"Right now?"

"It's urgent. He'll tell you about it on the way. Take a rope and hooks. People are trapped there, underground. We've got to get to them."

He did not mention that his son was among them.

"Of course, Pop."

"Take some bread and water. You might have a long way to go."

It occurred to me how terrified I, Givi, would have been at the thought of descending into some cold, dark cave, even for the sake of the trapped speleologists. But Beso had no fear; nor did I.

"I'll wait for you," said the old man.

The old lady stood on the porch. She handed me a pile of strong rope and a sack containing bread and wine. Then she made the sign of the cross over me and waited on the porch until we disappeared from sight. The puppy accompanied us to the gate, yapping his farewells.

"Is the post office open?" I asked Georgi.

"What do you need?"

"A telephone."

"The post office is closed, but Levan has a phone. Here's his house."

"Isn't it too early?"

"They're all up by now "

Georgi went in ahead of me. When I entered the house, its owner pointed to the phone and left the room immediately.

Georgi took the rope and sack from me and left the room, too, saying: "Dial eight first."

I called the institute. The information desk, downstairs. No answer. I had forgotten that it wasn't seven yet; the city started its day much later than Mokvi. I phoned the staff room, upstairs, certain that they had remained through the night, particularly after my disappearance.

Someone answered at once. It was Natella. I asked in a phony bass: "Can you please tell me the condition of your patient Beso Guramishvili?"

"Who is this, please?"

"His uncle."

I was afraid I'd be besieged with questions if she recognized me.

"Beso is a little better, but he's still unconscious. Is that you, Givi?"

Natella wasn't sure; she had inquired apologetically. I felt sorry for her.

"Yes, but I don't have any time now. Call you later."

I hung up immediately.

Georgi and Levan were waiting for me. "He's coming with us," said Georgi.

We turned off the road, hurried toward the mountains, and began to ascend along a trail. My companions walked quickly. The sun began to warm us, and I could hear my heart pounding from the exertion. But I knew I would manage to keep up with them, that nothing would happen to me. Still, I must start doing morning exercises; my life was too sedentary.

"I rose and forced myself to lean on my elbows. The evening star was shining above the spot from which I had just fallen. It was in the dead center of the opening, and although I realized I could scarcely reach the opening now, at least the star was a symbol of hope, a part of the bright world up above. I sat down. It was hard to breathe. No, not hard— impossible. I had to lie down and sleep. How long had it taken me to get here? Ten hours? One hundred? I probably

lost consciousness for several minutes, because when I opened my eyes again, the star had shifted to the edge of the opening. I pulled off my jacket; it only interfered with my movements. Now I would pause for breath and begin all over again. . . ."

"About five minutes more to the opening," said Georgi.

Shining like a silver band, the road wound far below us. Somewhere down there Beso had been found.

"No, I was found farther on. I lay on the ground. It was cold. It was late at night, and I didn't have the strength to raise my head to look at the star and thank it. The road was close by. A car passed, but I was too weak to shout. I tried to crawl down the slope. My hand wouldn't obey me, became tangled in my sweater, which was soaked with water or blood. I knew my temple was bleeding, but I couldn't do anything about it. I knew that someone would notice me if I managed to reach the slope beside the road. By following my tracks along the slope, they can find the opening in the mountain. At a slight slant on the other side of the road, there's a tree with a double crown. I'll lie on the slope and roll down like a log. I hope I don't lose Rezo's packet. It contains the balsam for his father. In the village of Mokvi, last house. And he's waiting for me there."

"Stop!" I said.

"Are you tired?" asked Georgi.

"Do you know these parts? Over there, down below by the road, there's a large double-crowned tree—"

They hesitated.

"Maybe by the turn?"

"No, there are two trees there. You know, by the—"

"Of course, over there."

"Then listen. Georgi, run back as fast as you can to the village and call the Brain Research Center. Tell them to drive to the place where Beso Guramishvili was found. And bring help— we've found the exit. Is that clear? Not to the exact spot, but to the tree with the double crown. There's a corkscrew turn there, and he rolled one turn lower. That's why they didn't find the exit. Got it? You, Levan, take me there, but slow. I'm very tired."

"Don't worry," said Levan. "It's downhill. Who was it that rolled a turn lower?"

"I told you already. Beso."

"But why didn't you know that before?"

"I couldn't remember it before," I replied, and tried to explain it to him as seriously and as thoroughly as Beso himself would have done. "Apparently it was much deeper in my subconscious, in a second layer of memory. Closer to my conscious memories—in the first layer—was Beso's last thought just before he lost consciousness. So I remembered about Pop Bagrat."

"What do you mean, *you* remembered?"

"OK, think of it as both of us remembering."

This Beso character was getting to be a drag. He was a good influence on me, and if I wasn't careful I'd end up turning into a nice guy, admired and respected by all who knew me. Natella would be delighted.

We descended along a narrow trail toward the road, which glittered like a slender winding stream beneath the rays of the morning sun.